A Baton Rouge Boss Saved My Heart 2

Published by S.Yvonne Presents

Interested in keeping up with more releases from S.Yvonne Presents? To be notified first of all upcoming releases, exclusive sneak peaks, and contest to win prizes. Please subscribe to the mailing list by texting Syvonnepresents to 22828

Previously in A Baton Rouge Boss Saved My Heart…

Kingston

I had been driving about twenty minutes with this bitch in the trunk and I turned up the music to drown out her muffled cries. I drove carefully making sure I didn't bring any unnecessary heat to myself. A few minutes later, I was pulling up to the old abandoned building on Weller Avenue. It used to be a church. The roof was damaged from Hurricane Katrina, and then in 2016 the building flooded from The Great Flood. JB had been using a portion of the old church to handle his business and shit. I don't even know how he got access to the building and I didn't ask any questions.

I pulled around back and checked my surroundings. The shit looks haunted as fuck. JB had brought me here a few weeks ago in case I ever needed a spot to handle some business. I got and followed the steps he showed me to get inside the building. I flicked the switch to turn the light on so I could see. I don't even know how the nigga got lights in this bitch but I'm sure it's illegal. There was a dingy ass mattress in the corner by the wall and a chair sitting in the middle of the floor. This was the perfect setup for what I had in mind.

I went outside, popped my trunk, grabbed the duct tape, and snatched MeMe's ass out. I could see the fear in her eyes and that shit was making my dick hard. Pulling her ass towards the building, I walked in and tossed her ass on the dirty mattress. I secured the building and hit the lock on my truck before walking back towards the bitch. I pulled the tape off her mouth, sat in the chair facing, pulled my gun from behind my back, and sat it on my lap.

"MeMe. MeMe. Long time no see bitch." I said as a fresh set of tears fell from her eyes.

"You don't have to do this. Kingston please just let me go and I promise I won't say anything to anybody." She begged as she ugly cried.

"Shut the fuck up bitch. I know you won't say anything to anybody cause you won't be walking out here alive."

"Please Kingston. If it's money that you want, I can get it for you. Think about what you're doing you don't wanna kill me and my unborn babies."

"Bitch, I don't need your fucking money and fuck them kids." I said pissed off at the fact that she thought telling me she was pregnant would move me. This bitch stole years of my life away and expects me to give a fuck about what she got going on. "That's a badass piece of ice you got on your finger. Too bad there won't be a wedding."

"Look Kingston since you're gonna kill me anyway, just go ahead and do it. Just know me and my babies will forever haunt your bitch ass," MeMe said trying to sound tough. Killing her now would be too easy but I plan to torture this bitch first. "Kingston you're the true definition of a FUCK BOY. You could never be the BOSS ASS NIGGA my fiancé is. You couldn't even be his store runner."

"SHUT THE FUCK UP BITCH." I said as I jumped out of my chair and backhanding her with the butt of the gun causing blood to immediately shoot out of her nose. She curled up in a fetal position on the dirty mattress shielding her face with her arm. I grabbed a fresh piece of tape, snatching her by her hair, and taped her mouth shut to muffle out her loud and obnoxious cries. I turned the light off and walked out of the building and locked it back up before getting in my truck and peeling off.

I needed to talk to JB, so I was headed to his house. Ten minutes later I was pulling up to his house on Glen Oaks Drive. This nigga was outside arguing with his ratchet ass baby mama La'Shunieceya who everybody calls LaLa, instead of trying to pronounce that ghetto ass shit. There was another chick. Lil mama was bad too. She was chocolate, thick as fuck with hazel eyes and a big ass curly afro standing off to the side like she didn't have time for the bullshit. I pulled in the driveway and sat in my car watching trying to figure out what was going on.

"Bitch get the fuck out my yard." He yelled at LaLa's ass.

"Nigga, I'm not going no fucking where till you tell me who this bitch is and what the fuck she doing here." She said pointing at the chocolate goddess.

"Look I don't have nothing to do with whatever this is y'all got going on, but you throwing that bitch word around a little too loosely. Make that your first and last time calling me out of my name." She calmly told LaLa.

"Bitch you are at my man's house, therefore you do have everything to do with this shit." LaLa clapped back at the chick and before I knew, chocolate drop was on her ass like a fly on shit. She dropped LaLa's ass with a two-piece and was bent over still throwing punches.

"Yo, Cuz. Help me break this shit up man." JB yelled out to me. I got out to help him get the girls separated, taking my time on purpose, enjoying the fact big bad LaLa was getting her ass beat. I couldn't stand that bitch. She ran off at the mouth too muhfuckin much. Once we had pulled them apart, he walked LaLa to her car and whispered something to make her drive off and leave.

"Sahara, I apologize for that shit. Disregard all that nonsense she was spitting. We are not together. I just happened to fuck around and knock up the baby mama from hell. You wanna wait inside for me while I rap to my cuz for a sec?" He told the chocolate beauty I now knew as Sahara.

"Oh, I'm not going anywhere. Besides, you owe me double for my trouble." She said walking towards the house.

"Nigga, who the fuck is that?" I asked once she was inside and had closed the door.

"She badder than a muhfucka huh? I been kickin` it with her for a few months now. One of them thots LaLa run with it spotted us coming out the store around the corner and by the time we made it to the crib, this bitch had whipped up behind us and that's when the shit popped off then you pulled up right after."

"Damn, what the fuck you gonna do?"

"Shit, I'ma smash what the fuck you mean?"

"Nigga, yo ass wild. But look I just wanted to let you know I got a lil issue tied up at the spot. I wanna torture em a lil bit before I send em to meet their maker." I said intentionally leaving out MeMe's name.

"Thanks for the heads up. Let me know when you need me to send the cleaning crew."

"Bet. I'm bout to get outta here and make a few stops before going back over there. Have fun with that in there." I told him as we walked back to my car.

"Oh, nigga I'm bout to have the time of my life. She got a badass friend I could put you on just say the word."

"I'm on good on that for now."

"Ya sure? I haven't seen or heard you mention any females since you been home. Let me find out you switched teams.' He said laughing.

"Man get the fuck outta here. Don't fucking come at me with that ol flugazzy bullshit. I been busy that's all. Just cause you ain't in the closet watching me fuck don't mean I ain't I getting no cut," I told his ass as I got in my truck and slammed the door.

"Man chill out I was just playing with yo ass." He said laughing like the shit was funny.

"Yeah, aight." I backed out of his driveway and made my way to the nearest hardware store. I needed to get a few things for the torture I planned to inflict on MeMe's ass later. Once I had everything, I needed from the hardware store I was back in my car to finish making the rest of my stops. My stomach growled reminding me that I needed to grab something to eat while I was out. I whipped in the drive-thru of the Popeyes on Airline and ordered me a three-piece mixed spicy, with a large order of red beans, and a large strawberry

Fanta with easy ice. I got my food and prepared to eat while driving back to the building where I had MeMe holed up.

I pulled to the back of the building and the first thing I noticed was the door was wide open. I threw my car in park, grabbed my gun as I got out, and made my way to the door unsure of what I would find.

"WHAT THE FUCK......." I yelled after flipping on the light switch.

Chapter One

Banga

I ain't plan for bro to find out about me and Shira the way he did, since I had already lied about the shit. Shira was face down ass up and I was balls deep when he hit me on my burner phone, so I knew something was up. I pulled out and went into the next room to see what was going on. He said MeMe was missing and he needed me to get somebody to drive her truck home. Since time was of the essence and I knew I couldn't just get anybody to drive the truck it made sense to have Shira do it.

"Say baby mama get up and get dressed as fast as you can," I told Shira as soon as I walked back in the room and grabbed my clothes to do the same.

"Get dressed? Nigga for what?" She sat up looking pissed that our session had been interrupted.

"That was TC on the phone and to make a long story short, MeMe is missing. He is waiting on us, so we gotta go right now." I told her and she quickly jumped up and started walking around in circles. "Baby mama. Get dressed. You wasting time walking in circles and shit. The fuck you tryna do, get dizzy before you get dressed?"

"Shut up, jackass. I was just trying to process what you said and think of who I needed to call first."

"We'll make calls after we pull up on bro. Let's just get there and see what the fuck we're dealing with." I told her as she was finally slipping her shoes on. We grabbed everything we needed and we jumped in my car and I sped off.

About ten minutes later, I was pulling up to the Rouses location TC sent me. I whipped in the spot next to MeMe's truck and threw my shit in park. I jumped out and walked around to let Shira out just as TC was walking towards us.

"Don't even say shit. I'll run it with ya later." I told him when he noticed I had Shira with me.

"Cool bruh. Sup Shira. Look, I need you to keep this between us for now. I need to talk to

Yah's folks first so no calls to your crew. Here are the keys. Let's head to the house, I've already wasted too much time in this fucking parking lot." He handed Shira MeMe's keys. We all jumped in our rides and pulled off and sped all the way to their crib.

Once we made it to the house, Shira called us over to help her unload the bags from MeMe's truck.

"Do we really need to be doing this shit now?" I asked grabbing a hand full of shopping bags.

"I just figured since she went grocery shopping and we don't know what she bought it made sense to bring it inside to make sure nothing spoils in her truck," She mumbled grabbing the grocery bags. Once we were all inside, Shira was putting the groceries up when out of nowhere she started ugly crying and shit. I guess it finally hit her that MeMe was missing.

"Come here, baby mama." I pulled her in my arms. "I know you're scared and shit, but now is not the time for tears. I need you to put ya big girl draws on and show me you a rider." I told her wiping her tears and kissing her on the forehead.

"I'm sorry y'all. I know me being hysterical isn't gonna help the situation. I've gotten it out of my system, so just tell me what y'all need me to do." She said as she looked over at me and TC. Damn, she bossed up quick as fuck, making my dick jump.

"It's all good. As close as y'all are, it's expected. I would have been looking at you sideways if there was no reaction at all," He told her looking her directly in the eyes.

"Now that we got that out the way, what's the plan bruh?" I asked to see what he had in mind.

"First thing first, I need to go to Yah's folks' house and let them know what's up. Ain't no way in hell I can tell them that shit over the phone. Besides mama Erycka, and Nique been blowing me up. Y'all wanna ride with me or follow me?"

"We'll follow you just in case we need to make a move. That way Shira will have my wheels."

"Bet. Let's ride out." He said grabbing both of his phones and YahYah's off the island. He locked up his house, set the alarm, jumped in his truck, and pulled off as we jumped in my car and did the same.

The ride to MeMe's people's house was quiet as fuck. Shira had a blank expression on her face as she stared out the window.

"We're gonna find sis. Even if we gotta paint the city red." I grabbed her hand and told her.

"I'm just worried and scared. Who would wanna kidnap MeMe?" She asked before her eyes got wide. "Oh my God. Do you think Kingston has something to do with MeMe's disappearance?"

"His bitch ass is at the top of the list, but we ain't confirmed the shit yet. Do you think that nigga really got the balls to pull that shit off?" I asked her while jumping on the interstate.

"I don't know, I mean I wouldn't it past him considering the shit he did before. I just pray y'all find my friend and bring her home in one piece. I don't care what it takes or how many bodies gotta drop. Promise me y'all are gonna find my girl."

"Say less. We gonna run in here, let her folks know what's up, then me and bro gonna hit these streets until we find her."

It took us about thirty minutes to get across town to Central where MeMe's folks lived. We parked, got outta the car, and followed TC to the front door. He rang the bell as we waited for someone to answer the door. I couldn't really read his expression, but I already know he is more fucked up about sis missing than anybody else.

Chapter Two

Tyzir

Since I was riding solo to Yah's folks' house, I made a call to Pete. I didn't wanna do too much talking in front of Shira. Everything isn't for everybody to know.

"Hey there TC, what can I do for you, my man?" Pete answered after a few rings.

"Sup my nigga? Yah's missing. Her phone, purse, and keys were left behind in her truck. So, I need you to help me locate her through the chip in her ring." She was so worried about that nigga coming home, plus she kept having those dreams, so I had to make sure I took extra precautions to keep her safe. Unbeknownst to anyone besides Pete, Ashad, and myself, I had some type of high-tech, top-of-the-line, micro-GPS, camera shit embedded in her ring. Pete assured me it was the best on the market.

"Oh my God. Are you serious?"

"Nigga, you think I would joke about some shit like that?"

"No, no man I didn't mean it like that. I just didn't think that we would really have to put the chip to use."

"Yeah, me neither. I got a feeling it's that nigga Kingston, but I'm not 100% sure."

"I'm on it. Give me a few minutes and keep your phone close by."

"Bet." I said ending the call so he can do his thing. I pulled up to Yah's folks' house a few minutes later. A sense of calmness washed over me as soon as I stepped outta my truck and I hope that was a sign that Yah and all three of my muhfuckin seeds was good. Banga and Shira followed behind me as I walked to the front door, rang the doorbell, and waited. A few seconds later, her pops answered the door with a shocked expression on his face.

"Hey, son, Osiris, and Shira. What brings you all by at this hour?" As he quietly observed us trying to figure out what's going on.

“Hey OG, I need to talk to you and mama Erycka. Can we come in?” I asked looking him dead in the eye to let him know this was serious.

“Hey old man,” Banga said not joking like he normally would about being called by his government name.

“Hey Mr. Carter,” Shira was trying to hold back tears as she spoke to him.

“Yes, come on in. We were in the sitting room waiting on you to call back with an update.” He said as we all followed him in the room where mama Erycka was sitting with the phone in her hand.”

“Hey mama Erycka,” I spoke up first while noticing the worried look on her face.

“Hey son, I’ve been trying to reach you. Hey, Shira and Osiris come over here and give me a hug, it’s been a while since I’ve seen you all.

“Hey Mama C,” Banga spoke as he and Shira walked over to hug her.

“Hey, Mrs. Carter. Yes, it has been a while.”

"Can I get you all something to drink or eat?" She asked as she stood ready to get whatever we needed.

"No ma'am we're good. I need to talk to you and OG about something very important." I said motioning for her to stay seated.

"Where's my baby TC?" She finally asked after surveying the room again.

"She's missing." I told them rubbing my hand over my face.

"Son, have you called the police?"

"Nah, you know them cops out here ain't worth a quarter. Plus it hasn't been forty-eight hours yet. I'd rather use my own resources than take a chance with them and end up behind bars or worse in a box."

"I understand. Fellas, let's go to my office and talk. We'll be right back love," he walked over to kiss her on the cheek. We followed Yah's OG to his office while Shira stayed behind with mama Erycka.

"Shira, how did you end up with the guys? Is there something I'm missing?" I heard her ask just as we rounded the corner as bad as I wanted to hear the response, I had more important matters at hand. Besides I think I had pretty much figured out that something was going on between her and Banga, I just don't know to what extent.

Once inside the office, OG went to the bar grabbed a bottle of Johnny Walker, poured each of us a shot, and passed it to us before taking a seat behind his desk.

"I didn't wanna get into the specifics in front of my wife. What do you know so far?" I ran down the entire scenario and how I was able to locate her truck and realize she was missing.

"I think that nigga Kingston might be behind this shit, to be honest. Given human trafficking is at an all-time high, I just don't feel like it was that. I got my tech guy working on trying to track her through her engagement ring and see if he can pull footage from Rouse's parking lot."

"What you mean tracking her through her ring bruh?" Banga finally spoke since we were in the office.

"Yah had been having dreams that Kingston had snatched her up ever since she found out he was getting out. Aside from sharing her location with me, I figured I needed to take extra steps. I'm glad I did since her phone and truck were left behind. I'm really depending on this chip I had placed in her ring when I got it customized."

"Son, that was good a damn good idea. Thanks for always having my princess's best interest at heart." Her OG said just as my phone started ringing.

"This Pete right here. I'm gonna put it on speaker." I told them before I answered the call.

"I got some information for you boss," Pete said as soon as the call connected. "I got Yah's dad and Banga right here with me. You're on speaker so go ahead and let us know what's up."

"I managed to access the security cameras from the parking lot and the focus isn't really clear.

From what I could tell, MeMe put the bags in the truck and walked away for a few seconds probably to put the shopping cart away. A tall male figure slipped into the passenger side of the truck and a few seconds later, she opens the driver's side door and just stands there. I'm assuming this is when she was told to put her purse and things in the truck because that's what she does next. The figure then walks around to the driver's side as she stands in place. Though I can't see it, I'm assuming he may be brandishing a weapon at her, which is why she didn't attempt to scream or run. He walks really close to her until they are out of the camera's view."

"Is it possible it's Kingston, son?" Her OG asked Pete.

"I couldn't confirm from the video footage alone sir. However, I was finally able to pull some data from the chip in her ring. I couldn't really see what happened as far as getting her in the vehicle. He drove around for a bit with the music playing loudly. He took her to another location. It doesn't look like a hotel or a large space, however, it does have lights. It looks like he tossed her on the floor because I could see he was sitting in a chair from the position of her hand. I think her hands are bound since the position of the camera doesn't move that much. I could hear her crying and she said some things."

"Well, spit it out nigga. What did she say?" I asked frustrated that he just stopped talking midsentence.

"I wasn't sure if you wanted me to disclose the conversation in its entirety."

"At this point, we need all the details we can get so we'll know how to move. You can proceed."

"After he removed what may have been tape from her mouth, I could hear crying and asking Kingston to let her go. She promised she wouldn't tell anyone and he yelled a few foul threats at her. She then asks if he wants money and that she can get it for him while begging him not to kill her and her unborn babies. He mentions the ring she is wearing and tells her there won't be a wedding. She tells him to just go ahead and kill her and that she and the babies will haunt him forever. He doesn't respond and I guess that made her mad because she let him have it and even mentioned you boss man. He yelled some more obscenities, jumped up, and struck her. I can't see where he hit her or if it was with his hand or an object. Her cries became muffled so he possibly gagged her or something. Then it gets dark and I hear the door close."

"So it is that nigga. Let's ride bruh, we gotta find my sis." Banga said jumping up from his chair so fast it fell backward.

"One sec, I got a few more questions before we slide."

"So, he's pretty much solo from what you gather? Have you been able to track her location? Do you think he took her ring?"

"I honestly think he's working alone. I haven't heard another voice and if there was someone in the car with him, they would have had to turn the music down to talk to each other. I have the location but I'm still working on trying to pinpoint the exact location. She still has her ring because if he had taken it, the location would have changed. I'm sending you a set of coordinates for the generalized location of where she is and hopefully, I'll have the exact location before you get there. You guys need to move fast. We don't know how long he's gonna be gone."

"We're on our way. Hit us up as soon as you get the rest of that intel. Let's slide bro."

"You need me to ride with y'all?" OG asked us as we were walking to the door?"

"Nah OG we got this. Just stay here with the ladies and please don't mention anything about the babies. Yah has this thing about waiting until she gets out of her first trimester before telling anyone." I told him as me and Banga damn near ran outta the office and to the front door. We jumped in my truck, my phone connected and the GPS boomed through my speakers with turn-by-turn directions. Banga grabbed my phone looking through the directions and said we needed to be headed to Weller Avenue. Instead of following the GPS directions I followed my own and took a shortcut to get there even faster.

Chapter Three

JuJu

I had pretty much gathered up my things in the cell without making it look like I was leaving. I just wanted to make sure I was ready when it was time for me to move. It felt good knowing Killa K had my back and was making power moves on my behalf. Since I had been steering clear from everybody for my own safety, I decided to lay in my bed and read my book. I had just turned on my side facing the wall as I read when I suddenly felt a presence behind me. I rolled over slowly and locked eyes with Kwik. My voice got caught in my throat as he stood there expressionless.

"Hey, is there something I can help you with?" I asked after finally finding my damn voice.

"Sup, nah bruh. You going somewhere?" He asked looking around the cell.

"N-No. I just did a little cleaning," I stuttered clearly showing how nervous I am.

"Were you molested or something?"

"Huh? Where did that come from?" I asked confused.

"I was just wondering, I always thought people like you were molested as a child or some shit like that?"

"That is just a dumb-ass stereotype and not my case at all, darling?"

"Chill on that darling shit. Well what's your story? How did you end up like that?"

"I apologize," I quickly said not wanting any smoke with him at all. "I was simply born in the wrong body."

"Born in the wrong body? What the fuck does that even mean?"

"Simple, I was born in a boy's body instead of a girl. I've always known since I was a kid."

"And ya folks cool with that?"

"I don't have any folks. I was left in an abandoned crack house when I was a baby and grew up in the system until I eventually ran away."

"Damn, so you didn't have any friends or anything like that?"

"Growing up in the system for a person like me is ten times harder than the average person. I was constantly taunted, teased, bullied, and beat up all because I was different."

"Why the fuck you run away?"

"Shit, what's the point of sticking around getting treated like shit and constantly not picked for adoption? Being a lil gay boy with pretty eyes and curly hair was not the idea of a son most fathers had in mind. They wanted a son to throw a football with and I wanted to play dress-up with my Barbie dolls."

"So, you ran away and lived on the streets?"

"Why all of a sudden you're talking to me and asking me all these questions?"

"No reason. It just seems like you terrified of a nigga or something and you stopped hanging outta the cell once ol boy left."

"I'm sure everybody in here who has heard a story or two about you is terrified. I've just been dealing with some personal stuff and been staying to myself lately." I told him because there was no way I was gonna tell him I miss my man and I damn sure wasn't about to tell him I was in here scared for my life even now.

"You ain't ever tried to find ya biological family?"

"Honestly, I never thought about it because I resented them. The fact I wasn't good enough for my parents or family to want me, made me not interested in them. Lately, I have been thinking that I wanted to find out who I am and where I come from. I feel I at least owe myself that much to find out the genetic history that makes up this gorgeous woman."

"Good luck." He cut his eyes at the last part. "Oh, I believe this is for you," he said dropping the missing letter from Killa K on my bed and walking off. This whole conversation has me confused as hell. I wanted to go after him and ask why did he have the letter, but my common sense and better judgment told me to leave that nigga alone and let him go on his merry way.

I sat back in my cell still trying to make sense of what the hell just happened. It seemed like he had done a complete three-sixty. I don't know what the hell Kwik got going on, but that shit he just pulled doesn't sit right with me. After a while, I finally got up to go to the phone and call Killa K. I called twice, but he didn't answer and I thought that was strange. I figured he was just busy and couldn't answer right now and made a mental note to call him after I got out of the shower.

I went back to my cell and grabbed everything I needed for my shower. I checked making sure I was alone since I still didn't trust anybody in the dorm. I got undressed and turned the shower on to where it was just the right temperature. Out of nowhere, I started feeling like I was being watched. I checked my surroundings not seeing anyone I figured I was just trippin' and went about my business. I had just closed my eyes and let the water run over me when suddenly a hand was covering my mouth.

"Don't move, don't try to scream or I will snap ya fuckin neck. Do I make myself clear?" The voice whispered in my ear, sending chills down my spine. I slowly nodded my head up and down clearly paralyzed with fear. "You thought you was gonna keep prancing ya lil pretty ass around here, with ya titties bouncing and shit like a nigga wasn't gon want a sample?"

My tears silently fell as they mixed with the water. I prayed in my head hoping that God could hear me as I braced myself for what I figured was about to take place. He spread my ass cheeks so wide, I can feel them ripping as he forcefully rammed his dick in me. My ass felt like it was on fire as he continued ramming me as hard as he could and I just continued to cry praying that it would be over soon.

"What the fuck going on in here?" Those were the last words I heard as I fell and everything went black.

Chapter Four

Mareyah

It seemed everything happened so fast; I went from having a mommy and me day, to being snatched up by Kingston's pussy ass. The shit happened so fast, I didn't even have time to react, otherwise I would have popped his ass and went home to cook for my man as planned. I am beyond terrified on the inside, but my priority is making sure my babies are ok.

My head was pounding and I am sure my eye is pretty much swollen shut after he hit me with that damn gun. Even with my hands tied behind my back, his lil bitch ass had to hit me with a weapon. I started praying harder than I had ever prayed before asking God to cover me and my unborn babies. I was in the dark, mouth taped up and I just prayed and prayed that TC or someone finds me before that nutcase comes back.

I can't believe my nightmares had actually turned into a reality. I wondered if my family had realized I was missing and was out looking for me. I already know I hadn't been gone long enough to even file a missing person report, so at this point, I'm depending on my family to come through and save the day. My goal is to remain calm and not bring any unwanted stress to my babies. I could hear noises outside and instantly froze, praying that he hadn't returned and the Lord had sent someone to save me.

The door slowly creaked open as a bright ass light was being shined in my face blinding me in the one good eye I had at the moment.

"Yah it's me, baby," TC said as he bent down and gently removed the tape from my mouth. I inhaled his scent and repeatedly blinked my eye just to make sure I hadn't fallen asleep and was dreaming. Hot tears poured out of my eyes as I realized my prayers had been answered.

"Thank you, Jesus." I finally spoke as he removed the ropes freeing my hands. I noticed Banga standing by the door shining the light towards us as TC looked over me and frowned when he saw my face. He picked me up bridal style and carried me out as he followed Banga and his choppa that led the way.

"You good now sis. We got you," Banga said as we made it to TC's truck. We got in the back as Banga hopped in the driver's seat. "Where to bruh?"

"She needs to be checked out, but we can't roll up to the hospital with her in this condition. For one, they gonna call twelve and two, our black asses will be their main suspects."

"Facts. Let me get Doc on the line and have him meet us at your house."

"Bet. Let me call mama Erycka nem and tell them the plan." TC said as I rested my head on his and held on to him for dear life. "Hey, mama Erycka we found her. Can y'all meet us at our house? We're headed there now."

"Thank you, Jesus." I heard my mom scream through the phone bringing on a fresh, new set of tears.

"Yes ma'am, we'll see y'all soon," He said before ending the call.

"Doc said he'll be there in about twenty minutes," Banga let us know as soon as he wrapped up his call.

"Yah, you're safe now." TC leaned over and placed a gentle kiss on my lips. "Did he touch you?" I shook my head no once it clicked that he was asking if Kingston had sexually assaulted me.

"I was so scared that I would never see you again." I whispered as the tears fell.

"I would have painted this whole fuckin state red before I let that happen."

"How were you able to find me since I didn't have my phone and wasn't in my truck?" He grabbed my hand and pointed to my engagement ring. "I don't get it, what about my ring?" He went on to explain how he had a custom tracking device installed in my ring as additional protection. I had no clue that he even had put Mark as my security detail, but he gave him today off to spend with his family.

"I hope you don't feel like I was trying to invade your privacy or that I went overboard with the security measures. I just wanted to make sure you were protected at all costs."

"Babe are you serious? That never crossed my mind. I'm just glad that you went above and beyond to protect me as best as you could."

"I told you, I got you and I always will."

"Hey, y'all. We're here." Banga yelled out as he pulled into the driveway. He got out of the truck, walking ahead of us to go open the front door while TC helped me out of the truck.

"Babe, I can walk," I told TC as he bent down to pick me up.

"And ya point?" He ignored me scooping me up.

"Nothing, I just wanna go inside and take a hot shower and wash the remnants of today off of me."

"It's your world babe. Doc will just have to wait and check you out once you're finished."

"Say, bro. Can you handle the door for me while I help Yah upstairs? When Doc gets here, let me know and I'll let you know when to send him up." He told Banga as soon as we walked into the house.

I immediately stripped out of everything once we were upstairs in our bathroom.

"You need me to do anything?" TC asked as he stood to the side of me.

"Nah, I'll be ok." I said as I walked further into the bathroom. I caught a glimpse of my face as I passed the mirror. I started the shower and turned the water on as hot as I could stand it and just let it run over me. In my head, I was replaying the events of today tears started falling as I broke completely down. I suddenly felt a cool breeze, then a pair of arms grabbed me from behind and for a second, I froze in fear until I realized it was TC. He pulled me into his chest, holding me tightly as he gently stroked my hair.

"Let it all out. I got you ma." He whispered in my ear. After crying my eyes out, I started to calm down.

"Babe why are you in here fully dressed?"

"Yah, I don't care about that shit. You needed me. I would walk through a blazing fire barefoot to get to you if I had to." He washed me up from head to toe and while I rinsed, he started peeling his clothes off. I reached down to grab his wet clothes before I left outta the shower but he stopped me. "Leave that shit there, I'll get it. Go ahead and get dressed. Doc is here and you need to get looked at." I left the clothes and made my way over to my hair supplies I grabbed some leave-in conditioner and applied it to my hair. I combed the conditioner through my air and brushed it up in a messy bun. I rubbed my body down with some mango body butter. I went over to the dresser and grabbed a bra and panty set. I grabbed one of TC's t-shirts and a pair of leggings. I got dressed and slipped on a pair of slides as I sat on the bed and waited on him to finish in the shower.

Chapter Five

Kingston

Where the fuck is this bitch? I said to myself as I stood in the middle of the floor trying to figure out what was going on. I know for a fact she ain't fuckin free herself and walk up outta here. I cut the lights off, locked the door, and called JB as soon as I was behind the wheel of my truck.

"Sup cuz?" He finally answered after the phone rang about three fucking times.

"Cuz you remember that lil issue I told you I had at the spot, right?"

"Yeah, what you changed your mind? You need me to pull up?"

"Nah but when I got back to handle the issue it was fucking gone. Do anybody else got access to it?"

"Get the fuck outta here bruh. The fuck you mean gone? Don't nobody have access but me and you."

"Like gone gone, without a fucking trace nigga. The only thing left was the rope and tape from their mouth."

"Oh, shit you fa real. You didn't have 'em tied up tight enough and they escaped or what?"

"I made sure the rope was tight as fuck. Ain't no way they just escaped. Somebody had to come in and untie em."

"Shit, what you gone do?"

"I'ma go home and try to figure this shit out."

"Nigga, this is crazy as fuck. Make sure ya keep ya eyes and ears open outchea in these streets and hit me up if you need me."

"Bet." I said ending the call as I headed home trying to figure out what the fuck just happened. Ain't no fucking way in hell her people could have found her. I made sure of that. That's why I made her leave all of her shit behind. Something ain't adding up but this ain't the end. I'm gonna get that bitch.

Looking at my phone, I noticed I had a few missed calls from JuJu from earlier but he ain't call back. I made it home about forty-five minutes later. That's the only thing about living in Gonzales, having to drive back and forth to Baton Rouge. I went straight to the shower once I made it inside. After washing up twice, I rinsed and got out and threw on a pair of basketball shorts, a wife-beater, some socks, and slides. I went to the kitchen and grabbed a Heineken and laid on the couch to watch some TV.

I must've fell asleep because the TV was now off and my dick was hard as a brick. I grabbed my phone to check the time and saw that it was a little after one in the morning. I ain't had no pussy since JuJu because I wasn't trying to cheat. I had been beating my dick since I came home and I needed to slide in something. I got up, grabbed my fitted hat and my keys so I can go take a ride.

I made it back to Baton Rouge in no time and decided to see if the rumors about Plank Road was still true. Plank Road has always been known as the hoe stroll, shit Scenic Highway too. I rode up the street and turned a few blocks to see if I could find any tricks. Trickin' ain't cheating and besides, JuJu will never find out. I circled a few more blocks before I saw a lil brown skin chic with a fat ass standing by the carwash. I turned off Plank Road on Chippewa Street turned right on Canonicus Street, and came up Osage Street, so I could pull on the side of her. I pulled my fitted over my eyes and let my window down. She pranced towards me and leaned in the window, once she was closer, I realized her face was a little stronger and nowhere near my type. This bitch ain't have shit on my JuJu but since I'm out here, I may as well do what I came out here to do.

"What's up? I like your car. Can I ride with you?" Her voice was damn near deeper than mine and she was trying to make it sound high-pitched.

"Get in." I said as she walked around and got in.

"I'm Phantaysia and I charge fifty for head and two hundred if you wanna fuck."

"Cool, you know somewhere ducked off we can go?"

"Yeah, I got you. What's your name?"

"My name ain't important. Where we going?" She called out the directions and we ended up on a dead-end street. "Ain't nobody gonna fuck with us out here huh?" I asked reclined my seat back and whipping out my dick.

"Nah we good nobody comes back here. Damn it's so big and pretty." She said reaching over and grabbing my dick and slowly jacking it.

"Quit playing with me and come show me what that mouth do." She started slowly sucking on it and it wasn't even good enough to be considered basic head. This shit was so boring I was getting sleepy. "Say ma get out and bend over the hood."

"What you don't like this?"

"Nah, I'm just short on time." I got outta my truck, whipped my dick out, slid a rubber on, and walked to where she was standing by the hood. I bent Phantaysia until I had her ass arched up just like I like it. I slid my in dick all the way and started beating them cakes up. I had my eyes closed and was in my own zone until it started feeling like she was doing something with her hand causing her to move and fuck up my rhythm. I opened my eyes and this bitch had pulled her dick out and started jacking off. My shit instantly with limp, I slid out madder than a muthafucka.

"Yo, what the fuck you doing?"

"Shit you was fucking me so good I wanted to cum too. Is something wrong?"

"The fuck you mean you standing out here jacking ya dick while I'm fucking you. I'm not into that gay shit. The fuck you thought this was?"

"The fuck, nigga you came on the block and whipped down on me, like you didn't know you was picking up a chick with a dick. Look just run me my money and drop me back off."

"I'm not paying for no trash ass head or them few seconds of smashing after you fucked up my nut. You got me fucked up. You better walk yo ass back." I said after I stuffed my dick back in my shorts. I quickly walked back to the driver's side, jumped in, and peeled off.

Chapter Six

Shira

I had been on edge ever since Banga told me about MeMe missing. I was still sitting here with her parents after TC and Banga flew out of here so fast. I called Monique and Shay to let them know what was going on. Monique and Cardell got here first and Shay and Darren arrived not long after them. We were all just sitting around making small talk trying to stay positive and remain calm.

"Um, Shira where is your car? How you get over here?" Monique loudly asked pulling everyone from their thoughts as all eyes fell on me.

"Monique if you don't use your inside voice in my house and mind your own business." Mrs. Carter said before I could say anything.

"It's cool Mrs. Carter besides they're gonna find out anyway. Banga and I are dating."

"You sneaky bit-."

"MONIQUE." Mrs. Carter cut her off.

"I'm sorry Auntie, you know my mouth don't have a filter. So, that's why his car is parked out front."

"You better find one in my house." She said as we all laughed.

"So how long this being going on and why was you keeping it a secret?" Shay asked giving me the side-eye.

"I'll catch all of y'all up at a later date, so I'll only have to tell the story once."

"Was it before or after the kickback?" Monique asked.

"After, why you asked that?"

"Cause, he kept calling you his baby mama. If it was before I was getting ready to cuss you out."

"Not in my house you weren't." Mrs. Carter said making us all laugh again. It felt good to see her in good spirits at a time like this. We all know how she feels about her MeMe. I couldn't really read Mr. Carter's facial expression, but he did appear much calmer after coming out of his office with TC and Banga before they left. Mrs. Carter's phone rang and she said it's TC and everybody got quiet.

"Thank you, Jesus." She screamed out loud as she jumped from the chair she was sitting in. It seemed like everyone released the breath that we were holding at the same time. "They found my baby. He said they're headed to their house and for us to meet them there." She told us once she ended the call with TC. Everybody started cheering and thanking God before grabbing our things and getting ready to leave. We all made our way to the garage. Mrs. Carter pressed the garage door opener so the rest of us could get to our cars in the driveway as she made her way to Mr. Carter's burgundy 2019 Mercedes Benz S-Class.

"Shay look how that heaux walking to her man's whip like she been driving it and shit." Monique loud mouth ass said just as I made it to the driver's side of the car.

"MONIQUE DE'SHAWN SCOTT-WILLIAMS." Mrs. Carter yelled at Monique clearly hearing what she had just said.

"My bad Auntie." She yelled back. "Dang she don't miss shit," she mumbled low enough for just us to hear and we all laughed.

I slid behind the wheel of Banga's car and adjusted to the seat and mirror before I backed out of the driveway. I turned on the radio just to get rid of the silence in the car as I was mentally preparing to go see my girl. I prayed she wasn't hurt or anything, but I also had to be realistic and be prepared for anything since we didn't have any details right now. Once I made it to MeMe's house, I realized I must have been driving faster than I thought since I beat everybody else there. I got out and took a deep breath and released it before walking to the door and ringing the doorbell.

"I see you made it baby mama. Is my car still in one piece?" Banga asked as he opened the door smiling. Lordt this man is just too damn fine and his gold grill was just the icing on the cake.

"Boy please, I can drive. Everyone else should be pulling in soon. How is she?" I asked praying it wasn't too bad.

"She's a little banged up from what I could see. She went upstairs to get cleaned up. Doc just went up there to examine her and should be wrapping that up in a minute."

"Has she said anything or mentioned who did this?"

"Nah she didn't say much on the way here or before she went upstairs, but sis is strong as fuck and she'll back to herself before we know it.

"Alright, you folks have a good evening and call me if you need anything." The man who I assumed to be Doc said as he came downstairs holding a large medical bag.

"Thanks again bruh and I will be dropping your payment in your account in a few minutes," TC said as he and MeMe came into view shaking his hand before he made it to the front door.

"Good looking out my nigga. I already took care of the payment bruh." Banga said like a boss.

"Hey friend, how are you holding up?" I walked over to MeMe and hugged her.

"I'm okay friend," she said holding her head down.

"Unt Unt friend pick your head up. You are still beautiful no matter what," I told her when I noticed she was embarrassed about her face. Her right eye was swollen shut and purplish-black and there was a dark bruise on her face just a little to the right of her eye and her cheeks were flustered and red. I didn't notice anything else other than what looked like rope burns on her wrists. "What did the doctor say? I asked her as I followed her into the kitchen.

"He told me to apply cold compresses to my face to help with the swelling and to call him if it worsens or starts to bleed. Besides that, he just told me to get some rest."

"I can take off tomorrow and come sit with you and keep you company if you need anything."

"Awww thanks, friend, but you don't have to miss work. Plus, you know and I know TC won't be letting me out of his sight no time soon."

“You damn right I’m not,” TC said as he and walked in to let us know everybody else had made it. We left out of the kitchen to go join everybody else in the den.

Chapter Seven

Tyzir

Whoever came up with the portable ultrasound machine or whatever it's called is the muthafuckin MVP. Once Doc confirmed that the babies were all fine, I let out the breath I didn't even know I was holding. I looked up at Yah and she smiled at me. She was just as relieved as I was that they were not harmed and had survived this crisis.

Once Doc left, we were all in sitting in the den so we could fill everybody in and answer any questions they may have. MeMe was sitting in between her folks her mom was holding her so tight as she rocked back and forth rubbing her back.

"Ok love, that's enough give her a little room to breathe." Her pops told mama Erycka.

"I'm just happy my baby girl is sitting here all in one peace. Not everyone gets a happy ending like this." mama Erycka told him loosening the hold she had on Yah.

"It's ok mommy. I'll like to go ahead and get this conversation over with and put it all behind me. First, thank you all for coming out to check on me and making sure I'm ok. Kingston is the one who kidnapped me. He had me tied up inside some old and rank abandoned building. He hit me in the face with the butt of his gun. Thank God that's all he did before he left me there. I'm just glad TC took the extra steps to keep me safe and was able to find me using my engagement ring." She looked up at smiled at me.

"I got you forever." I told her as I winked at her.

"That bastard did this to you? I'm gonna call the police and see to it that he's behind bars again. This time for the rest of his life messing with my damn baby girl." mama Erycka said and we all looked at her in shock.

"Mommy. I didn't know you had it in you." YahYah said in shock.

"Chile please, I wasn't always saved just ask your daddy. I don't play about my family especially my baby girl."

"Ooooh daddy you ain't never tell me mommy had a little ratchet in her." She looked over at her pops and said while smiling.

"That's a different conversation for another day."

"Well after today's events, I figure that we can end it on a positive note." Yah got up and walked over to where I was standing and grabbed my hand. "I really wanted to wait and plan something special to tell you all this, but oh well I'M PREGNANT." She yelled out as I grabbed the frame that was placed face down on the table next to me.

"MAREYAH ME'YHANA CARTER you looked me dead in my face and lied to me, little girl." mama Erycka screamed as she jumped up and made her way to us.

"I'm sorry mommy. I really wanted to wait until my first trimester was over before we told anyone."

"It's fine baby. I can't wait to start shopping for my first grandbaby. How far along are you?"

"I'm almost ten weeks and but there's more." I flipped the picture frame around so they could see the ultrasound pictures from her first appointment.

"Triplets..." Her pops yelled out before hugging us both. "Congratulations to you both."

"Daddy, you're not mad, are you?"

"Princess for what? Girl, you're grown and damn near married." He said waving her off. One by one everybody made their way over to congratulate and hug us and/or dapped me as they congratulated us. Banga walked over last and everybody got quiet.

"Why y'all got quiet all of a sudden?" Banga asked looking around.

"Cause we know you bout to say something off the wall," I told his ignant ass.

"Well, all y'all wrong. I just wanted to say welcome home sis and congratulations on y'all bundles of joy." He said with a straight face. "My nigga hit ya with a three-piece, BOW." This fool yelled out while he did a lil popular Baton Rouge dance called Jiggin. That's where Baton Rouge got the nickname Jigga City from.

"Since we revealing secrets, Shira got one too." Monique yelled out causing everybody to look over at Shira.

"Didn't I tell you to mind your own business?" mama Erycka asked Monique as she popped her upside her head.

"Dang Auntie you didn't have to hit me that hard. I was just reminding her."

"Well, the only people who don't know at this point his MeMe. I'm sure TC connected the dots or found out tonight. Anyways Banga and I are dating." Shira said all in one breath.

"That's how you let the world know you my baby mama? You are something else." Banga said shaking his head.

"Oh, you sneaky, sneaky, sneaky little cow. I can't say what I wanna say in front of my parents. One question was I right from the jump?" Shira's faced turned beet red.

"You ain't even gotta answer that your face told it all, but congratulations to y'all. Banga, you better treat my friend right."

"What about me sis? You ain't gonna tell ya friend to treat me right?" This fool had his hand on his chest like he was appalled with Yah. We all sat around laughing and talking a little while longer before everyone finally left after saying they would check on Yah tomorrow.

"What you wanna eat bae?"

"I don't really have an appetite, but I already know you're gonna make me eat something. I'll take a club sandwich, some chips, and a pickle on the side."

"Say less. Go in there and relax. I'll let you know when it's ready."

Chapter Eight

Kingston

JuJu hasn't been the same since his accident the same day I had snatched MeMe's ass up. Mr. Renzetti called me first thing the morning after and ran the shit down to me. Some nigga raped my girl in the shower and she hit her head when she fell or something, but she ended up with a concussion and having to get stitches in her ass. She ended up being in the infirmary for about a month. When I finally talked to her, she said she only heard his voice but never saw his face. The last thing she remembers hearing is Kwik's voice asking the what the fuck going on or some shit like that. In her mind, Kwik saved her life, which confused me because the day before she claimed he was trying to kill her.

I had been chilling since the night of that MeMe bullshit. I still don't know what happened, but I decided to fall back for now. I'm pretty sure her people got a close eye on her for now, but they'll eventually let their guards down and I'll be ready to make my move. JB had still been trying to hook me up with one of Sahara's friends. I figured it was beginning to look weird since I had been home and no one has seen me with any females. Besides JuJu hasn't been the same since and she barely calls or writes.

It was about six o'clock when I made it to JB's house, I got out and knocked on the door.

"Sup, cuz?" He answered the door and let me in the house.

"Shit, I can't call it. Where the girls at?"

"Sahara just called and said they should be pulling up in a minute."

"I hope her friend ain't bullshit. I could use me a lil yeah with the yeah."

"I'm telling you she official like a whistle."

"Yeah, nigga she better be." I told his ass right before somebody knocked on the door.

"Sup, bae?" He asked as soon as he opened the door.

"Hey boo." Sahara walked in and said before kissing him. She looked even better than the last time and I hoped her homegirl was just as fine.

"This my cuz Killa K. Killa K this my girl Sahara."

"Hey, I know damn well your mama didn't name you no Killa K, boy what is your real name?" Sahara asked with her hands on her hips.

"It's Kingston." I told her laughing at her lil feisty ass.

"That's better. Kingston this is my friend Burgundi. Burgundi this is Kingston and you already know JB." Sahara said introducing us.

"Sup Burgundi." I said liking what the fuck I was seeing. She wasn't as thick or as dark as Sahara, but just as fine with the big, natural hair thing going on. She gotta smooth, caramel complexion and pretty ass hazel eyes. She gotta nice lil slim, thick frame with perky A-cup titties and a flat stomach. She ain't gotta lotta ass but a nigga can work with that.

"Hi Kingston nice to meet you."

"So y'all decided what y'all wanna get into tonight?" JB asked them.

"Bowling." Sahara shouted like she had been waiting on him to ask.

"Bet. Where we going Metro Bowl?"

"Nigga Metro Bowl been closed down for a minute. Y'all wanna go to Quarters?" JB asked everybody.

"Yeah, Quarters is cool plus we can hit up The Grind after we finish playing." Burgundi answered with a smile.

"Well shit let's be out. Who riding with who?" JB asked as we all made our way out the door.

"I'm riding with you boo and Burgundi and Kingston can ride together that way they can get to know each other."

"I'm cool with it if lil mama is cool with it." I said looking over at Burgundi.

"That's fine let's roll." She followed me as I led the way to my car and opened the door for her before I got in on the driver's side. I waited on JB to pull off so I can follow him since I don't know shit about no damn Quarters or The Grind.

"So, what kind of music you like?" I asked her as I connected my Bluetooth to my truck.

"I'm more of an R&B chic, but I like rap too."

"Well, here you find something for us to listen to." I passed her my phone and she put on some Jhené Aiko chic's *Trip* album. "What is this you got a nigga listening to?"

"You never heard of Jhené Aiko? Just listen to a few songs and if you aren't feeling it you can change it. It has a nice lil vibe to it just give it a chance."

"Bet. So, what's to you?" I asked trying to get a feel of lil mama.

"Well let's see I'm an only child. I'm from St. James Parish. I recently graduated from The Southern University with a double major in Biology and Chemistry, and I work as a Clinical Research Specialist at the Pennington Biomedical Research Center. How about you?"

"Oh, you one of them smart chics huh? I fucks with it though. Well, I just came home from doing a bid for some bullshit. Been pretty much laying low and getting back to the money since I came home."

"Getting back to the money huh? What do you do?"

"I'm a boss baby nothing more, nothing less. You got a man, kids?" I asked changing the conversation.

"Trust me if I had a man, I would not be here with you. No, I don't have any kids yet, but one day in the future I'll have a nice lil family. What about you girlfriend, kids?"

"Nah, lil mama I don't have no attachments. So, what do you like to do for fun?"

"I like to read, exercise, travel, shop, cook, and hang out with friends. You?"

"I'm a homebody baby, work and home. I hang out every now and then, but the club thang ain't never really been my scene. Ya feel me?"

“Well, it looks like we’re here.” She said looking up as I pulled up in the spot next to JB nem and parked.

Chapter Nine

Mareyah

It had been a few months since that whole fiasco with Kingston. For a while, I was terrified about going anywhere especially alone. It took a while, but TC convinced me to get out of the house more. He even bumped Mark up to my driver/security, which was even better since most days I didn't even feel like driving.

I was now sixteen weeks pregnant and I am amazed at how big my belly has grown. Thankfully, besides my breast being fuller and ass being a lil fatter, I am all belly. My cravings are out of this world and my emotions are all over the place. I gotta brag on my man though. TC has been hands-on with my pregnancy, waiting on me hand and foot, and dealing with my emotional ass like it was nothing. We had finally decided on which room would be the babies nursery, but we wouldn't start decorating until after my gender reveal. I really didn't want a gender reveal, but my mom wants to do it and she announced it at the small but over-the-top dinner party she threw for my birthday. TC was cool either way so once we were at the appointment, we had them put the gender in an envelope and seal it.

I had just finished getting dressed so I could hit up a few boutiques and get a mani/pedi. I called Mark to let him know I was ready and would be down in a few minutes. I needed to find something to wear for my gender reveal and upcoming maternity pictures. It had become a challenge to walk downstairs and always wears me out so TC put a chair next to the staircase for me. I sat for a few minutes before walking in the kitchen, grabbing myself something to snack on during the ride and a bottle of water. I locked up, walked to Mark's truck and he got out to help me in the backseat.

"Good morning MeMe."

"Good morning Mark. How's it going?"

"Everything is everything. Where to first?" I told him the name of the boutique I wanted to go to first and pulled out my phone to call TC.

"Good morning babe." I greeted him once he answered.

"Morning bae. What ya got up this morning?"

"Mark's taking me to a few boutiques. I need to find something to wear to this damn gender reveal and a few things for the maternity pics. Once I'm finished, I'm gonna go get a mani/pedi and that's about it. How's work?"

"That's what's up, you know I don't like you staying cooped up in the house anyway. We a little short-staffed so I'm gonna help out in the kitchen for a bit."

"I know. I try to get out but these babies take all of my energy and I'm always sleepy. I love how you don't mind helping the staff even though you're the boss."

"I know baby. It'll be over before you know it. Shit, it's a small thing to a giant plus you know I like to get in the kitchen anytime I can."

"Well, you can get back to work babe. I don't wanna take up too much of your time. I was just calling you before I get my day started. Let me know what you want for dinner so I can cook once I'm done."

"Ok bae and don't overdo it. You're pregnant now with triplets so you can't be zipping around like you used to. As for dinner, I got that covered you don't need to be on your feet like that."

"Well, alrighty then, I'll talk to you later. Love you."

"Love you too."

I went to the first boutique and didn't see anything I liked. After going to two more and ending up with the same results, I decided to either get something made or order something online. I had Mark take me to the nail salon for my mani and pedi. The pedi was so relaxing I dozed off and didn't realize it until Ling Ling was gently shaking my shoulder to wake me up. Once I was finished, I decided to call in me a food order for lunch. I asked Mark if he wanted anything, but he declined as usual, so I called Willie's and placed an order for a seafood potato and a club salad with ranch dressing.

Once we picked up my order, I told Mark I had no other stops and that I was ready to go home. I got comfortable in the backseat and took another nap on the ride home.

Once again, I was being gently shaken from my sleep. This time it was Mark letting me know we had made it to the house. He helped me out of the truck and carried my food as he walked me to the door. I thanked him, grabbed the bags, and headed straight to the kitchen. I placed my food on the island, washed my hands, and sat down to stuff my face. I closed my eyes, swinging my feet as I enjoyed my first bite of potato. This one of my favorite things on their menu and it tasted like it gets better every time I eat one.

"That's a damn shame." TC said standing in the doorway laughing at me causing me to jump.

"Babe, you scared me. What are you doing home so early?"

"One of the night cooks called in asking if he can come in early for some overtime, so I didn't have to stay as long as I initially thought. How did shopping go? Did you find anything?"

"Well, that it sounds like that worked out well. No and no. I might just order something online or get something made. Oh, that reminds me I saw some furniture for the nursery that I wanna show you to see if you like it."

"You know I'm cool with whatever Yah. Have you decided on what color furniture you're gonna go with or are you waiting for the gender reveal for that too?"

"I know babe, but I still wanna get your input. That's why I think that gender reveal shit is stupid. A baby shower would be more than enough but you know how extra my mom is."

"Let her have her fun babe. These are her first grandbabies."

"What you mean first? Shit, these are her last too."

"Oh really? You don't wanna have more babies later on down the line?"

“I can maybe do one more once these are at least five.”

“I can dig it. A total of four or five isn’t too bad.” He said smiling wide.

“Whatever.” I told him as I continued to eat my food.

Chapter Ten

Banga

Things were slowly getting back to normal after we got sis back. Me and my baby mama was doing good. I can't even front having a girlfriend ain't all that bad. To be honest, I was tired of slanging dick all across the city, but shit nigga got in-house pussy on speed dial now, ya feel me. That lil pussy got some power. I done cut off all my hoes. She be having a nigga agreeing to do all kinda crazy shit. Like right now she gotta nigga dressed like some fucking cotton candy for MeMe's gender reveal. What the fuck is a gender reveal? Who even came up with that shit, people come up with any excuse to throw a fucking party?

"Say baby mama you ready to go?" I called upstairs to Shira who came down in a short set matching mine. One side is light blue and the other is light pink since we are team boy and girl.

"Yeah bae, I'm ready if you are."

"Shit let's slide. I'm ready to get my eat and drink on. You know MeMe folks' parties be kinda lit to say they some old folks."

"They sure do. I wonder what's on the menu today."

"Come on greedy ass so we can find out." I told her slapping her on the ass when she walked by."

"You better chill out. You know I like that freaky shit."

"Shit say the word and we can go back upstairs. They can just call us and tell us what they're having."

"Boy bring yo ass on here. We ain't missing this. You know everybody always clowning us saying we be late for everything since we started dating."

"That be yo ass always wanna get a quickie in after a nigga get dressed and shit. I keep telling you I am not a piece of meat."

"I like how you flipped the script when it's always yo ass initiating the quickies, Mr. Let Me Just Get A Lil Sample To Hold Me Til Later."

"You are something else. You ain't gotta bring up old shit." I told her as she grabbed her purse off the counter before walking to the garage. I grabbed my keys and followed behind her. After I locked the door, we hopped in my 2020 GMC Sierra sitting on twenty-six-inch Forgiatos. I barely drove this muthafucka, especially with these raggedy ass Baton Rouge roads. I done lost count on how many times I had to replace my fuckin rims.

"You did remember to grab the gifts, huh?"

"Well, it's a fine time to ask when we halfway there, but yeah everything is in the back. They really told everybody to just bring diapers and wipes. I'm not the smartest muthafucka but I know a baby needs more than just diapers and wipes."

"Smart ass. I meant to ask before we left but you distracted me talking about quickies and shit. Yeah, this is just the gender reveal so it's common to request just diapers and wipes. They are having triplets so can you imagine how many diapers they are gonna need?"

"Oh yeah, you do gotta point."

"Besides I'm sure her registry will have everything else on it for the baby shower."

"Damn, so there's still a baby shower too?"

"Yeah, what you thought the gender reveal was it?"

"Shit yeah. I tell you what, I'm not dressing up like no damn cotton candy for the next event."

"You don't look like no damn cotton candy. I think our outfits are cute. You don't like em?"

"They aight." I said not wanting to start a fucking argument cause a nigga wanted some pussy later.

"Oh, that's what I thought." She said side-eyeing me. It took us about forty minutes to get to MeMe's folks house and there were cars everywhere. I found a spot as close as possible and parked. I grabbed the door handle to get out and Shira did the same.

"Girl if you don't get your hand off that damn door. I done told you about that shit. You don't open doors around me."

"My bad bae I'm so used to doing it."

"You better get unuse to it. I ain't them lame ass niggas you used too."

"Whatever come on here before we're late." I got out and walked around to the other side to help her out of the truck. "You need me to help with anything?"

"Shira you better stop playing with me. I wish you would try to lift on one of these heavy ass boxes."

"I was just trying to help you out smart ass. I'm going inside."

"So, you ain't gonna wait on a nigga and hold the door open for me? You are something else." I told her shaking my head before going to let the tail gate down and grabbed one of the large boxes loaded with cases of diapers. I could only carry one at a time because they are heavy as fuck. We didn't think this shit through. We bought three cases of each size of diapers and fifteen cases of wipes.

"You got it, bae?"

"Yeah, I'm good baby mama. Lead the way." I followed behind Shira as she walked around to the backyard where the reveal was taking place.

"This is so beautiful." She said as soon as she opened the gate.

"Yeah, this shit is dope. Doesn't even look like a fucking backyard."

"Osiris. You better watch yo mouth in my house." mama Erycka said appearing out of nowhere.

"My bad mama Erycka. How you doing?"

"I'm good son. Hey Shira, how are you?"

"Hey, Mrs. Carter. I love your dress."

"Thank you and your outfits are cute. How did you get this one to cooperate?"

"It took just one threat and he was on board." She said as they laughed.

"Mama Erycka where do you want me to put these? I have more in the truck to get." I asked her ready to put these boxes down.

"Over here follow me. I'll show you to the gift table."

"Hey everybody." I yelled out as we walked further in the backyard.

Chapter Eleven

JuJu

I haven't been the same since the attack. I felt broken and a shell of the person I used to be. I still don't know who it was, but if it wasn't for Kwik ain't no telling what else would have happened to me. I didn't see my attacker's face, but I will never forget that voice. For weeks I couldn't sleep because I would hear his voice in my dreams. I was moved to a different dorm once I got out of the infirmary, but I had just been staying to myself. I blamed Killa K for what happened to me and even slacked up on calling and writing him. I know it's wrong because he ain't have shit to with what happened and has been nothing but good to me. I got up to make a call to my lawyer to see if there's any update on my case.

"Hello, Mr. Renzetti. How are you?" I greeted him after he accepted the call and it connected.

"Hey there Miss Chavez. What can I do for you today?"

"I was just calling to see if there are any updates with my case."

"Actually, there has been an update, and things are working out in your favor. I have a meeting this afternoon and I expect a good outcome. I'll follow up with Mr. Francois after to keep him updated on what's going on."

"That sounds great. I'll be praying on the inside while you work your magic on the outside. Also, I did think about that other issue and I would like to proceed with that."

"I'm so glad that you decided to go forward with it. I will begin working on that first thing in the morning."

"Great, thank you so much. Also, can you keep this issue between us? I'd like to tell Kingston on my own time." Mr. Renzetti had previously advised me to take action and file a lawsuit against the prison for my rape attack. I finally decided to move forward with it, but I wanted to deal with it on my own. I'll tell Killa K about it when I was ready to do so.

"You're quite welcome and I definitely understand. I need to get ready for my next appointment. I will update Mr. Francois this evening if you would like to follow up with him."

"Sounds like a plan. I will do just that. Have a great rest of your day sir."

"You too, talk to you soon. Bye." I decided to give Killa K a call since it had been a while since I had heard his voice. I called and the phone just rang until it rolled over to voicemail. I decided to try again before going to my cell, this time he answered.

"Sup, bae?" He answered once the call had connected.

"Hey boo. How are you doing?"

"I'm good. How bout you?"

"Honestly, I'm doing better. I just talked to Renzetti and he said things are looking good."

"That's what's up. Did he say anything about you getting out anytime soon?"

"No, but he did say he has a meeting later on and he will call you after to update you."

"Word. I hope it's good news. I can't wait to have you home with me."

"Yeah, me too. Bae, I just wanna apologize for how standoffish I've been towards you. I just needed a moment to get my head together."

"It's cool ma. You had a traumatic experience and it's normal to not feel yourself."

"I guess you're right. So, what have you been up to?"

"Nothing much really. Handling business and shit with my cuz JB."

"That's what's up. I miss you and I can't wait to see you."

"I miss you too and hopefully it's sooner than later." The operator announced one minute left and he told me to call him back tonight to find out what Renzetti had to say. I agreed, ended the call, and walked back to my cell."

Once back in my cell, I decided to go out on the yard. It had been a while since I went outside. I figured I needed some fresh air and had been cooped up in here long enough. I stood up against the fence and just let the sun shine on me for a minute. I had been standing with my back against the fence for a while before some of the girls came over. We were just standing around making small talk when all of a sudden, I felt like someone was watching me. Figuring it was just my nerves, I brushed it off and continued laughing and talking to my girls.

I couldn't shake the feeling that I was being watched and began to look around when my eyes met this big ass nigga from my old dorm named Menace. I always thought he was weird since I never heard him say anything but I had caught him staring at me on multiple occasions. It was something about the way he looked at me this time that just made me feel really uneasy. I don't know what it was, but something about him that was really rubbing me the wrong way. After breaking eye contact, I discreetly asked the girls if they knew anything about this weird ass nigga and they said rumor has it he's some kind of serial rapist or some shit like that. The revelation made every hair on my neck stand up and the wheels in my head started turning.

I just needed to hear his voice. I don't know how I was gonna pull that off, but I had an idea and I knew just the person who could help. I couldn't wait until I talked to Mr. Renzetti and tell him my thoughts. For now, I would watch my back and not give out any indications of my suspicions. I went back to my cell and grabbed my things to go take my shower. My plan was to come back and relax until it was time to call my man back.

Chapter Twelve

Tyzir

Mama Erycka went all out for YahYah's Twinkle Twinkle Little Star themed gender reveal. I tried to help cover some of the expenses and neither she nor OG would have it. I made a deal with them though, I let em have their way with this one and let em know I would foot the bill for the baby shower. I understand that Yah's their only daughter, but she's my woman, carrying my seeds and I can handle the costs. I told her once she gets the theme from Yah, she can go crazy and there is no limit or budget.

There had been so much food I don't even think I had a chance to try everything. I wasn't worried though mama Erycka had already said she was sending us home with some of everything. I was standing off to the side talking to Banga and some of the other fellas while the women were sitting around mingling with each other. The DJ announced it was time for the big reveal. I nodded my head letting him know I heard him as I walked towards Yah. I helped her out of her seat and walked her to the area designated for the gender reveal as everyone gathered around us. There were three large boxes decorated to match the Twinkle Twinkle Little Star theme with the words Baby A, Baby B, and Baby C on the top of each one lined up next to each other. We are supposed to open the boxes and the balloons will float out and tell us what each baby will be.

"On the count of the three, you will open the first box." The DJ announced as everyone got ready to see who was right.

"ONE, TWO, THREE.." Everyone yelled as we opened Baby A box. We looked at each other confused as one large black balloon surrounded by a bunch of blue and pink balloons floated out of the box.

"Mommy, what does this mean?"

"It means y'all having a black baby." Banga ignant as yelled out causing everybody to laugh.

"Baby girl it means the answer is in the black balloon." mama Erycka said as she walked over and gave us both a pushpin while cutting her eyes at Banga's dumb ass. "I had to make it a little more challenging for you guys." She said smiling.

"Alright you guys on the count of three." the DJ yelled out again.

"ONE, TWO, THREE...." Yah and I both pushed a pin in the black balloon at the same time and blue confetti fell out.

"IT'S A BOYYYYY..." The crowd screamed out as we got ready for Baby B's box. We went ahead and opened the box assuming we would have to pop the black balloon inside it as well. The DJ got everybody ready to start the countdown again.

"ONE, TWO, THREE...." They all yelled out again, we popped the balloon and once again blue confetti fell out.

"IT'S A BOYYYYY...." The crowd yelled again. I looked over at Yah and noticed her facial expression had changed a little. Despite her saying that she didn't care about the gender I know deep down she wants at least one to be a girl.

"Alright, y'all it's time for the last one..." The DJ yelled out. We opened the last one and I grabbed Yah's hand.

"It doesn't matter what's inside the balloon, as long as we have three healthy babies that's all that matters." I whispered in her ear as she nodded her head and smiled.

"ONE, TWO, THREE...." They yelled for the last time and we popped the balloon as the pink confetti fell out.

"IT'S A GIRLLLL...." The crowd screamed as Yah smiled while tears rolled down her face. I pulled her emotional ass in for a hug and kissed her temple.

"You good bae?" I asked her.

"Hell yeah. I got me a mini-me out the deal. I was good either way as long as they are healthy.

"Girl bye. You should have seen your face after that second balloon." I said teasing her. One by one everyone started walking up congratulating and hugging us.

"Two boys and a girl. I was praying for us bruh. The Lord heard my cry." Banga stupid ass said when he got close to me.

"Praying for what fool?" I asked while laughing at his crazy ass,

"Nigga, I was praying that it wasn't all girls. You know how many lil niggas we was gonna have to knock off when they got older?" He asked with a serious face.

"Damn, I didn't even think about that shit. We still have one and she ain't dating till she makes forty."

"Sure, in the fuck ain't. Hell, fifty might even be better."

"Hey, can you guys start sitting the gifts out? It's time for MeMe to start opening them." mama Erycka walked over to me and Banga and asked.

"Yes, ma'am. Any particular spot you want them?" I asked her.

"Yeah, can you place them around the throne chair she's gonna be sitting in?"

"I thought everybody brought diapers and wipes. What she need to open them for?" Banga asked the question I had in my head.

"Osiris, though it was requested, not everyone brought just diapers and wipes."

"I asked Shira if we could bring other things besides diapers and wipes and she told me no. She said the gender reveal is just diapers and wipes. I swear she is something else." Banga said shaking his head.

We walked over to where the gifts were set up and started doing what mama Erycka had asked us to do. We moved just about everything and the only thing left was big asses boxes filled with wipes and diapers.

"Man, just leave them heavy ass boxes right there. Ain't nobody tryna keep picking that shit up. Just know all that shit is diapers and wipes from me and Shira." Banga said making sense when I thought about how many more times they would have to be moved.

"Word. I appreciate it bruh. Y'all ain't have to do all that."

"Man hold that noise that's my nephews and niece. This is just the beginning. I wish Tee Delaney and Ma was here to see this shit." He said dapping me up.

"Yeah, man me too. I wish they were here to see how we turned out." I said as I looked out and focused on Yah opening her gifts.

Once Yah had finished opening up the gifts and had taken a million pictures, we grabbed the mic from the DJ and gave a thank you speech to all of our guests. I told Yah to get off her feet and have seat while we started loading up all of the babies' gifts. I should have rented a damn U-Haul as I started looking around at all the shit we would have to load up. By the time we finished loading everything up, we had a whole damn entourage trailing us home with baby stuff. I can honestly say these babies are extremely blessed and this is just the beginning.

Chater Thirteen

Kingston

I had been kicking with Burgundi for a lil minute nah. She was cool as fuck and a good look since everybody wanna be in a nigga business and shit. I had been by her crib more than a few times and she had asked when I was gonna invite her to mine. I wasn't sure if I wanted to do that just yet especially since JuJu might be coming home soon. I was headed to pick Burg up since her cousin was having a cookout or some shit and she wanted a nigga to go with her. I started to tell her no, but I have been thinking on ways to make this shit work in my favor. I figured she can be my girl I can be seen with in public and JuJu can be my girl tucked away at the crib.

I pulled up to Burg's crib and got out to go let her know I'm here since she probably ain't even ready yet. Burg has a nice lil three-bedroom, two-bath, brick house in Mayfair East, with a cute lil flower bed in the front, and a nice lil deck in the backyard. Shorty is definitely on her shit and a nigga was kinda feeling her too. I rang the doorbell, stood on the porch, and waited for her to answer.

"Hey, handsome." She said smiling as she opened the door.

"Sup, Ma?"

"Come on in, I just need to slip my shoes and I'll be ready."

"Bet. Damn them shorts got that ass sitting right." I told her as I slapped her on the ass following her into the house.

"Whatever. You know my ass sits right regardless."

"Shit, I can't argue with that." I took a seat on the couch and waited for her to go change her shoes."

"King, can you come here for a sec?" I got up and went into her room to see what she wanted.

"Sup?"

"Which shoes should I wear?" She was wearing a pair of short white denim shorts and a light purple Ralph Lauren Polo t-shirt. Her shorts were short but not ass hanging out the bottom short. I looked down at her feet she had a cute lil light purple open-toe sandal on one and a purple and white Vans slip-on on the other.

"They both look good but my choice is the sandals." I'm a sucker for pretty feet, especially when the toes are polished white so of course a nigga chose the sandals.

"Well, sandals it is." She said changing the other shoe.

"I was thinking instead of driving back to Baton Rouge after leaving from by your people, why don't you pack a bag and stay the night with me?"

"You sure? I don't want you to feel rushed to invite me over."

"It's cool shorty. Besides I think it's time I bring you into my world."

"If you insist. It won't take me long to pack." Ten minutes later I was walking out holding her bag as she followed behind me stopping to set her alarm. I went ahead and put her bag in the back of the truck while she locked up her house. I walked to the passenger side and opened the door for her before going to the driver's side and getting behind the wheel. Once I started up the truck, she put the address in the GPS, and I passed her my phone to find us some riding music.

Forty minutes later we were pulling up to some big ass house in Grammercy with cars lined in the driveway and all the way down the street.

"Your people must be pretty breaded up. This house looks like a damn mini-mansion."

"My cousin's husband is a chemical engineer so I guess you can say they're doing alright." She said and smiled.

"Alright my ass, them people balling."

"Let's get outta here. I'm starving." I got out and walked around to open her door. I hit the locks as we walked towards the backyard where everybody was. She introduced me to a few people as we made our way into the yard. "Hey look there's my cousin over there. Come on so I can introduce you."

I followed her as we walked to where her cousin was sitting and I almost passed the fuck out.

"This is my cousin Sascha and her husband Drayke. Sascha this is my boyfriend Kingston. This is her house and the host of the party." She said introducing me to her cousin who was the spitting image of MeMe and kinda favored JuJu too. I guess that shit is true that everybody has a twin but in this case triplets.

"Sup, y'all." I finally spoke to them as I shook their hands.

"Well don't be a stranger there's plenty of food and drinks. We have boiled, baked, fried, and grilled food. You name it we got it and if we don't, we can go it." Drayke told us as he walked towards a large cooler.

"What all y'all boiled?" Burg asked her cousin Sascha.

"Shit, just about everything blue crabs, shrimp, crawfish, snow crabs, corn, potatoes, and meat."

"I think that's what I wanna start off with. You want boiled food or something else?" Burg asked me as we walked off to go get some food.

"I'll take a lil boiled meat, fried and grilled food."

"Well come on and I'll make you a plate before I fix mine."

I walked with her to go wash our hands before we went to the table with the fried food.

"You see anything you want?" She asked looking at all the food spread out on the table.

"Yeah, let me get a couple of pieces of that fried catfish and a piece of fried chicken too. Where the sides at?"

"They're on the table behind the grilled food. Come on we can go that way now. What else you want?"

"Shit, let me get two of them BBQ ribs, one of those shrimp skewers, and that's good on the meat a nigga needs some sides now and I'm good."

"Cool come on. If you don't eat anything else, you gotta try Drayke's chicken and sausage jambalaya. It is so good and one of the best I've ever had."

"Well, fix a nigga a little of the jambalaya, baked beans, and some of that green salad with Italian dressing."

"I'll grab us some drinks and we can go find us some seats. You want a beer or a cold drank?" She said once she had fixed my plates and handed them to me.

"I'll take a Heineken."

"Got it. Come on let's grab a seat."

"Thanks, shorty. What you doing with a Dos Equis?"

"I like to drink them when I'm eating boiled food. Look, there's two empty seats under that tent over there." She pointed out. I followed her to the table, sat my food down, pulled out both chairs before sitting down and opening my beer.

"Hold my seat, I'm going get my food. Do you still want boiled meat?" Burg asked standing next to me."

"Yeah, you can bring me a lil something.
told her right before she walked her fine ass off to go get her food.

I can't lie, Burg's people were cool and it seems like everybody gets along. We sat around playing cards, dominoes, throwing horseshoes, and some drinking games. It was a little after eight. Burg's ass was lit from all them Patron shots and was getting real touchy-feely in front of her folks, so I knew it was time to go. I grabbed her a bottle of water as we made our rounds telling everybody bye. Once I got her strapped in the truck, I walked around, hopped in, and put Trey Songz's *Anticipation* album on before pulling off.

It took us about twenty minutes to get to my house since Gonzales wasn't that far from Grammercy. I pulled into my garage, grabbed her bag off the backseat, and walked around to help her out of the truck. Once we made it inside, I told her to make herself at home while I took her bag upstairs. She had taken her shoes off and was sitting on the couch flipping through the TV channels when I came back down.

"You good lil mama?"

"Yeah, why you ask?"

"Cause yo ass was lit before we left from by your people."

"That was light work. I only had a few shots. I can handle my liquor."

"I got something else you can handle." I told her with a smirk.

"You already know I can handle that too."

"Say less. Shit, you wanna come take a shower with me?" I asked her standing up and reaching out for her hand.

I led her upstairs to my bedroom and she went to her bag and got her body wash and some other shit before following me to the bathroom. I stripped down, grabbed some face towels, and started the shower. She stripped down, grabbed her body wash, and got in the shower with me.

We stood under the shower as I kissed her sliding my tongue in her mouth. She let out a low moan as we kissed each other deeply. I pulled away and trailed kisses down her body, I slightly lifted one of her legs and dove headfirst in the pussy. I had smashed Burg a few times before but this was my first time tasting her. She tasted like fresh peaches and I knew a nigga was gonna be hooked. I slid two fingers in as I continued eating the pussy like it was my last meal.

"Oooh Kingston" she lowly moaned my name.

"You like that shit?"

"Yesssssssssss."

"Go ahead and cum for me." I told her as I continued working my fingers inside her and massaging her clit with my thumb.

"Shit, I'm bout to cummmm." She moaned and I switched my fingers with my tongue. I was ready to catch everything she had to offer and that's just what I did. Once, I was satisfied, we washed up, rinsed, dried off, and went straight to the bedroom.

I laid her on the bed and grabbed a rubber out of the nightstand next to my bed. I rolled it on my dick before laying down and motioning for her to come ride this dick. She slowly slid down until she was fully adjusted and then she went crazy on my shit. I wasn't ready to nut yet so I tapped her on the ass to get up and let me hit that ass from the back. Once I had her face down, ass up, and arched just the way I like it, I slid back in. I held her ass cheeks wide open with both hands as I slid in and out of her wetness and hitting her spot.

"Where you going? Bring that ass back here." I asked as she tried to run from the dick down, I was giving her. I took one hand, slapped her lil ass cheek, and it wiggled just a little bit. I guess lil booties do matter and then I zoomed in on her asshole. It was so pretty and clean, I pulled my dick out and went face first in her ass. I ate her from front to back and back to front before I slid my dick back in. I massage her asshole with my thumb as I stroked her slowly.

"Burg, you like how that feels?"

"Yessssss, please don't stop."

"You gonna let me open that backdoor tonight?" She froze and tensed up.

"I told you I'm not into anal sex."

"It's cool ma." I told her as I closed my eyes, speeding up my strokes pretending I was in her ass instead of her pussy.

"KINGSTONNNNNNN." She yelled. I had zoned out and was beating the pussy out the frame.

"My bad bae, did I hurt you?"

"Slow down. You got too rough and it was hurting." She looked back and said with tears in her eyes.

"My fault." I pulled out and laid her on her back. "Let me kiss it and make it feel better." Once I felt like I gave her enough tongue action, I slid back in with long, slow strokes. "You gonna cum with me?" She nodded her head unable to speak. I could tell by the fuck faces she was making she was about to cum, so I sped up my strokes and bust right after. I got up, went to the bathroom, pulled the rubber off, and flushed it. I washed my dick off, grabbed a warm soapy towel, and washed Burg off.

Two minutes later she was knocked out sleep. I got in the bed and just laid there thinking about JuJu before I fell asleep.

Chapter Fourteen

Mareyah

I had been shopping like crazy since I found out the gender of the babies. Everybody had been telling me to slow down so people will have stuff to buy for the shower, so I focused more on the nursery furniture and décor. I decided on a classic Snoopy theme using the colors black, white, gray, and yellow. I wanted a bold, black accent wall with white trim which TC and Banga insisted on painting. I ordered three gray matching four-in-one convertible crib changing tables, dresser, and chest sets. Each crib will have the same Snoopy bedding but I'm gonna get the blankets embroidered with their names so they won't get mixed up.

Once I found all of the matching mobiles, wall art, stuffed animals, and any other décor I could find, and ordered it. I'll order the wall signs with the babies' names once we decide on them.

"Hey bae, what you up here doing?" TC asked as he walked in the bedroom making his way towards me. He leaned over to give me a quick kiss before he started taking off his shirt.

"Hey, babe. Nothing much just ordering stuff for the nursery. How was work?"

"Work wasn't bad at all. The new hires are catching on and keeping up. I should have known you were in here ordering stuff."

"That's great. Yeah, I wanna make sure the nursery is completed before the baby shower, so it'll be easier to put everything up. When do you and Banga plan on painting?"

"It's all good bae. I'll get with him and see when he has a free day. I'll grab some swatches while I'm out tomorrow so you can pick out which shade of black for the wall and the white for the trim you wanna use. In the meantime, did you get everything you needed for the maternity shoot?"

"Cool beans. Yeah, I got everything I needed and I ordered your stuff as well so we're both squared away. Time is moving fast before we know it, we'll have three babies down the hall."

"Yeah, it is. If I had it my way, I'd make you my wife before they get here."

"Aww, babe. Everything happened so fast and I just didn't have time to plan a wedding. Plus, I'll be too fat to wear my dream wedding gown. We can just go to the courthouse if you want and have a wedding later."

"You ain't said nothing but a word. Pick a date and set that shit up. Stop calling yourself fat. You are carrying three little people and even though your body is changing, you're still beautiful as ever."

"I'll jump on that first thing in the morning. You're right. I have three little people growing inside of me. Sometimes I can't even believe it's real. Did you bring me anything to eat?"

"Yeah, it's downstairs. I'll go get it for you."

"Thanks, babe. No, go ahead and take your shower. I need to get up and stretch my legs anyway. I'll go downstairs and get it."

"Yah it's nothing, I'll go get it."

"TC I'm not crippled. I can handle going get my food. You better go take your shower or you won't be getting none tonight." I told him as I grabbed my phone and got up.

"Well since you put it like that, to the shower I go."

I slid my feet in my slippers and made my way downstairs. I had to sit my fat ass in the chair for a minute when I got down there. Then I had to pee so I went straight to the bathroom once I got up. After relieving my bladder, I washed my hands and made my way to the kitchen to see what he brought me. Whatever it was I could smell it as soon as I walked into the kitchen. My mouth started watering as I lifted the lids off the containers of baked turkey wings, cornbread dressing, yams, mac & cheese, and green beans. I fixed enough food for me and the babies to make sure we all got full. I grabbed me a bottle of water out of the refrigerator before sitting to say my grace and digging in.

"OMG, this is so good." I said to myself after eating half of my food.

"That's a damn shame. Yah open your eyes and quit talking to yourself."

"Huh?"

"Ain't no huh. I saw your little greedy ass in here talking about some OMG this is so good with your eyes closed and feet swinging." He told me as I fell out laughing.

"Hush. I didn't even hear you come in. You always sneak up on me when I'm eating."

"That's 'cause you were too deep in your plate. You good or you need something else?"

"Yeah, once I finish this, I'll be good for a while. I'm gonna want some fresh fruit later though. Do you want me to fix you a plate?"

"No, go ahead and feed my seeds. I'll fix it and I'll get your fruit together after I eat." He fixed his plate and pulled up a seat next to me at the island. We sat around making small talk as we ate. Once we were done, I got up and grabbed my plate. "Leave it Yah. I'll take care of it. What are you about to do now?" I sat the plate back down on the table.

"I'm going in the den and find something to watch. I've been upstairs all day and I don't feel like going back up there just yet."

"I told you just because you're at home, you don't have to be cooped up in the bed all day. I'll be in there in a sec after I clean up these dishes and wipe down."

"I know babe. I was so busy focusing on the nursery and time just passed me by. Is there anything, in particular you wanna watch?"

"Nah, I'm good with whatever you choose."

"Ok." I went into the den, grabbed my favorite throw blanket, and got comfortable on the couch. I flipped through the channels and stopped on *Chopped.* TC got me hooked on this show, so I already know he's gonna want to watch it. I've been telling him to look into seeing how to get on the show, but he said he just doesn't have time to do it. We stayed downstairs for a while and I ended up falling asleep as usual. I woke up and told TC I was going up to shower and asked him to bring my fruit upstairs.

After my shower, I sat up in bed while TC laid across my lap, feeding me fruit, and barely watching some movie on Netflix. I bit into the juicy chunk of pineapple TC had just put in my mouth causing the juice to quickly run down my chin. He immediately licked it off and began planting soft kisses on my neck intentionally blowing on my spot causing the floodgates to open. He moved the bowl of fruit to the nightstand, pulled off his t-shirt before crawling in between my legs, spread them as wide as possible, and began eating the soul out of my pussy. My breath was caught in my throat for the first few minutes, I couldn't even moan.

"You good up there?" He pulled back and asked.

"Yessssssss." I said finally finding my voice. Satisfied with my response, he dove back into my wetness. He was eating the pussy like Winnie the Pooh eats the honey out of the jar.

"Oooooohhhhh shitttt. I'm about to cummm." I moaned loud as fuck.

"Let that shit go Yah." He said and just like a switch had been flipped, my juices came flowing out and he lapped up every drop. That was the last thing I remember before I was out like a light.

The next morning, TC was already gone when I woke up. I got up and wobbled to the bathroom to relieve my bladder and take care of my hygiene. I grabbed my phone, laptop, and made my way downstairs. Once I caught my breath, I took my laptop in the den and then went to the kitchen to find something to eat. I checked the microwave first to see if he had made me breakfast before he left. My eyes lit up as I saw the plate of cheese grits, scrambled eggs, and sausage links. While my food was warming up in the microwave, I fixed myself a glass of orange juice and pulled out the freshly cut bowl of fruit.

After I had finished eating and washed my dishes, I grabbed my fruit, went to the den. Fruit was one of my biggest cravings and I literally ate them all day every day. I started making calls gathering all the necessary information regarding getting married at the courthouse. Once I wrote down all the information, I curled up on the couch for a nap.

TC was walking in just as I was getting up to go use the bathroom.

"Sup, Ma?"

"Hey babe, give me a sec. I gotta go pee." I swear these babies stay on my bladder. TC was sitting in the den when I finished, I climbed in his lap to give him a big juicy kiss. "You're home early."

"Yeah, I didn't have much to do besides inventory. I see you made it downstairs. What you got into today?"

"I called around to get all the details about getting married at the courthouse. Here's all the information right here." I told him as I passed him my notepad.

"Ok, that seems simple enough. I know Banga is gonna be my witness and I'm pretty sure Nique will be yours. We just have to pick a date that works for everybody. I got the swatches for the paint in the car. I'll grab them in a second. You feel like getting out the house for a little bit?"

"Yeah, I think Nique is the better choice and it makes me not have to choose between Shay and Shira. I already know my mama's extra ass is gonna put together some kind of celebration after I tell her our plans. Ok, that's good. The sooner I pick the shades the sooner y'all can get to painting. Yeah, I can use some fresh air what you got in mind?"

"You trust ya man, right?"

"Without a doubt."

"Well let's go upstairs and get changed into something comfortable before we slide." Once we were dressed and ready to go, we made our way downstairs. TC locked up the house and I walked to the car. After helping me in the car and getting in the driver's seat, he passed me the swatches and we were on our way. A little while later we had pulled up to Mae Lah Maternity Boutique on Jefferson Hwy.

"What are we doing here?" I asked confused as to why we were here.

"Well, if we're getting married, you're gonna need a dress?"

"Yeah, but it's bad luck for you to see me in my dress before the wedding."

"Follow me. I have an idea." He said before getting out and coming to help me out of the car. We walked into the boutique and the sales clerk greeted us as soon as we walked in and asked if she could help us find anything.

"Hello. Yes, you can this is my fiancée and she needs a nice little dress for our wedding. Can you please help her find something since I'm not allowed to see her in it before the wedding?"

"Sure thing sir. I would love to help. Come right this way ma'am and congratulations on your wedding and bundle of joy." The sales clerk replied as she smiled at us.

"Thank you so much and it's actually bundles of joy. I'm having triplets." I told her causing her to get even more excited.

"Looks like you'll be in good hands. I'll be outside in the car bae. Call me when you're ready to check out." TC said before walking back out of the store.

Chapter Fifteen

Banga

I was up early as fuck since I agreed to help TC paint the babies nursery. A nigga was up all night fucking around with Shira's ass. I literally fell asleep in the pussy, so I woke up this morning and started stroking some mo. She's downstairs fixing a nigga something to eat while I hop in the shower. I can't be out here painting on an empty stomach and with no energy.

Once I was finished with my shower and hygiene, I threw on a white t-shirt, some old white pants, and white Reebok classics. Looking like a damn professional, I grabbed my phone and made my way downstairs. Shira was just sitting a plate of scrambled eggs, bacon, and sausage links on the table next to a small bowl of fresh strawberries before going back into the kitchen. She came back with two glasses of orange juice and sat down across from me.

"Damn, baby mama this looks good as fuck. I'm just glad you're ain't one of them chics who can't do shit but order food and make reservations. A nigga like home-cooked meals more anyway."

"And ain't. My mama and grandmothers kept me in the kitchen. You'd be surprised at what I can do."

"Well in that case what you cooking tonight for dinner?"

"Boy bye. I'm your girlfriend, not ya personal chef or ya wife."

"You are something else. Am I not worthy of a good home-cooked meal?"

"Yeah, you're more than worthy of it but I'm just not obligated to cook it for you."

"I'm appalled. All this good dick I've been slanging and I can't even get a meal."

"Whatever, Osiris. Eat before your food gets cold." She said picking up her fork.

"Bow your head lil heathen and say grace."

"I got your lil heathen asshole." She said grace and dove into her food.

"I can't even front this shit taste good too. I hate when food be looking all good and then bite into it, the shit be nasty as fuck."

"I told you I know my way around the kitchen."

"The jury's still out on that I need to sample something other than breakfast."

"You tried it."

"What you got up for the day?"

"Nothing much I'm going back to sleep when you leave, then I'm going home and straighten up my house a little bit."

"I don't know why you just won't move in here." I told her being serious.

"Move in? Don't you think it's too soon for that?"

"Says who? Wverything we have done up to now has been on our own terms. It just makes more sense. You're always here or I'm always at your house so clearly we like having each other around."

"You do have a point, but can I think about it first?"

"Yeah, you can but if you take too long or choose wrong, I'll just decide for ya."

"What does that even mean? How can you decide for me?"

"If you take too long or decide wrong, it really don't matter. I'll have the final say." I told her as I winked.

"Whatever Banga." She said with an attitude. She finished up her food and snatched up her plate.

"Oh, I'm Banga now." She flipped me off and went into the kitchen.

I heard the water running and figured she was in there cleaning up. I finished my food and took my dishes to kitchen. I stood behind her rubbing my dick against her ass while I put my dishes in the sink.

"Do I need to take ya upstairs and fuck that attitude outta ya before I leave?"

"I don't have an attitude." She said rolling her eyes.

"If you say so. I'm bout to slide before TC starts blowing up my phone. Give daddy a kiss before I go." She turned around to kiss me and I slipped my tongue in her mouth deepening the kiss the way she liked it. I bit her lip a little before pulling away.

"Asshole." She said laughing.

"Aight, baby mama, I'll hit you up later to see where you at. I'm out." I scooped up my phone and keys, making my way to my car. I hopped in and turned on that old Lil Boosie *Bad Azz* album. That bitch still go hard. I pulled off and drove the fifteen minutes to TC's house.

I pulled up and called him to let him know I was outside. I didn't wanna ring the doorbell in case MeMe was still sleeping.

"Sup bruh?" He answered.

"I'm outside come open the door."

"Bet."

"You ready to get this shit over with?" I asked walking in the house dapping him up.

"Hell yeah. I'm surprised your ass on time. You know you be late for everything since you and Shira started fucking around."

"Damn, we show up to a couple of events a few minutes late and nobody lets us forget the shit." I walked off shaking my head.

I stopped off in the kitchen and grabbed me a bottle of water before following him upstairs to the nursery. I was glad he had already started taping off the wall and didn't have much left to do. Once we had the paint ready and the floor covered in plastic, we got to work. We made small talk while we painted and I must say the shit was looking good as fuck. It's been a minute since a nigga painted but shit, we still got it.

"How's the relationship thang going bruh?" TC asked with a smirk.

"It's all good. I asked her to move in with me this morning."

"Not Mr. Fuck Em and Duck Em. What did she say?"

"Y'all like bringing up old shit. She said she needed to think about it."

"Word? What you think her answer's gonna be?"

"Shit, it really doesn't even matter. I already told her if she takes too long or chooses wrong, I'll decide for her."

"How are you gonna decide for her foo?"

"Easy. I'll just send a moving company over there to pack up all her shit and bring it to the crib. Problem solved."

"Nigga, yo ass is crazy. Keep me posted on how that shit plays out." He said laughing like I just finished telling the joke of the year. "Before I forget, me and Yah decided to just get married at the courthouse and I need you to be my best man."

"Say less my nigga. Just give me the date, time and I'm there." We finished up the first coat of paint and decided to start putting the furniture together while we waited for it to dry.

"Man, I really appreciate you coming through to help me out today. It probably would've taken me a couple of days if I would have done it solo." He told me as we walked across the hall to the room with most of the boxes of baby furniture in them.

"I told you bruh, these my nephews and niece so it's nothing. You know we was raised to stick together and that's just how that shit go."

"Big facts. Man, Yah ain't play no games with this furniture shit. This a nice lil setup." He said looking at the boxes of what it's supposed to look like when we get finished.

We got busy putting together all of the cribs first before going to add another coat of paint. MeMe came in and asked if we were hungry, so we went downstairs to eat the sub sandwiches and chips she made for us. It was dark outside when we removed the tape from the wall after the paint dried. We cleaned up everything and moved the extra paint before carefully putting the furniture in there while MeMe directed on us how she wanted it set up. The nursery was coming together nicely and it's not even finished.

"Aight y'all. I'm bout to slide." I told them once we were done.

"Thank you for coming over today and helping bro."

"Sis, you don't have to thank me. Shit, we family."

"I know but you gave up your whole day to help TC and you didn't have to do that." She said tearing up.

"It's nothing sis. Please don't start crying."

"Shut up big head. I can't control these damn hormones."

"It's ok sis." I told her giving her a quick hug. I leaned down to her belly to talk to the babies. "Uncle Banga is about to head out and go home. I'll talk to y'all soon." Her belly starting moving in different directions.

"Babe look the babies are kicking." She pulled her shirt up so we could see.

"Man, what kind of exorcist shit is this?" I swear I saw footprints.

"Banga get your crazy ass outta here hyping my babies up." MeMe said laughing as they continued to kick.

"Hey, daddy babies, give ya mama a break. Y'all Uncle Banga doesn't know no better." TC said laughing when he stood up.

"So y'all gonna act like y'all ain't see them footprints in her stomach?"

"It's natural foo." TC said and MeMe was laughing so hard she was crying.

"Aight, I'm gone. I'ma tell my baby mama how y'all treat a nigga over here. One L."

"One L bruh."

I heard him respond before I walked out the front door and hopped in my car. I called Shira to see where she was. Since she was home that's where I was headed. All a nigga ready to do is shower, eat and lay up for the rest of the night.

Chapter Sixteen

Shira

I went back upstairs to sleep after I finished cleaning up the breakfast dishes and wiping down everything. I set my alarm and was knocked out soon as my head hit the pillow. My screaming alarm scared me out of my sleep. I sat up and stretched before getting up to make the bed up. After making the bed, I went into the bathroom to take care of my hygiene and shower. Once I was done, I threw on a t-shirt, a pair of shorts, and some flip-flops and grabbed everything I needed before going downstairs. I set the alarm and hopped in my car headed to my house. I stopped by Burger King and got myself a Whopper Jr with cheese meal, onion rings, and a Coke since I hadn't eaten since breakfast. I ate my food while driving and was finished by the time I made it home.

I went straight to the kitchen to pull out something to cook. I had a taste for lasagna so I pulled everything out I needed before I got started cleaning up my apartment. I didn't have much to clean since I had been at Osiris' house damn near all week. I cleaned both bathrooms, did a few loads of laundry, vacuumed and mopped. Once I had everything clean and smelling all fresh, I lit my favorite strawberry and lemonade candles to make it smell even better in here.

It was a little after six so I decided to go get started on my dinner. I poured myself a glass of Stella Rosa Moscato D'Asti, connected my phone to my Beats Pill, and went into the kitchen to start cooking.

"Sup baby mama? Where you at?"

"Hey, bae. I'm at my house. Why?"

"Bet. I'm on my way." Osiris's rude ass said before disconnecting the call. I had been toying around with the idea of moving in with him. I was trying to outweigh the pros and cons but still felt like it may be too soon. I hope he doesn't expect an answer tonight when he gets here cause I damn sure don't have one yet.

"Damn it smells good in here." He yelled walking into the kitchen where I was pulling the lasagna out of the oven. I sat it to the side and put the garlic bread in the oven. The whole kernel corn was done so I turned it off. "I see you changed ya mind and cooked for daddy."

"Boy bye. I cooked for myself you just happened to come over." I said trying to hold my laugh in.

"Ya period on?"

"No, why you ask me that random ass question?" I asked him as I pulled the garlic bread out of the oven and turned it off.

"Shit gotta make sure you ain't tryna get a nigga with that red sauce. Now that I think about it, we've been fucking around for a minute and I don't remember you ever saying your shit was on. What's up with that?" He asked and I froze like a block of ice. "Baby mama, you good?" He asked snapping his fingers in my face. I snatched my phone off the counter and opened up the Glow app. According to the calendar I haven't had a period since the week before the kickback at MeMe's house.

"No, no, no, no, no." I kept saying over and over as I paced the floor.

"Shira, what the hell is wrong with you?" He asked grabbing my arms to stop me from pacing.

"I haven't had a period since before the first time we had sex."

"And ya point?"

"I think I need to take a pregnancy test." I nervously told him.

"Say less I'm bout to run up the street to Walgreens and grab one. I'll be right back." He grabbed his keys and literally ran out of the house. I sat on the couch and stared blankly at the wall. Before I knew it his ass was walking back in the house with a bag full of pregnancy tests.

"Don't you think you went a little overboard with the tests?"

"Shit, I didn't know which one to get so I got two of each. Come on let's go see if I made you my baby mama for real."

"You stay your ass right here. I'll be back." I said snatching the bag out of his hand, grabbed a plastic cup out of the bathroom, and made my way to the bathroom. Once inside I closed and locked the door. I read over the directions for each test before getting started.

"You are something else. Why you locked me out? That's my baby too."

"Shut up jackass. I haven't even taken the test yet."

"I don't need a test to tell me I done knocked you up. That pussy has been gripping my dick tighter than usual. Look in the mirror, that ass done got fatter and them hips done spread too. Let me go call my bruh and tell him the triplets bout to have a playmate."

"You better not call nobody and say shit. I'm about to take these tests and confirm I'm not pregnant." I yelled at him through the door. He acting like Martin on that episode when they thought Gina was pregnant. Hopefully, I get the same results. I used the plastic cup to pee in which made it easier to either dip the tips of the test and to use the dropper for the other tests. I wiped myself and pulled my clothes up. Once I had all the tests lined up on the counter, I washed my hands and sat on the toilet, and waited the necessary time before checking the results. It didn't take long before the same results popped up on each test. I stood in place not knowing how to feel.

I opened the door and Osiris damn near knocked me down.

"Well, what did they say?" I was speechless and walked clean out of the bathroom. Before I made it to my bedroom, he was in there screaming like a damn fool. "I told y'all niggas. I told y'all niggas. My baby mama is officially my baby mama." I made it to my room as the tears silently rolled down my face.

A few minutes later he walked into the room looking at me confused.

"What's wrong bae? Why you crying? You not excited?"

"I honestly don't know how I feel. I mean are we even ready for a baby? Don't you think this is too soon?"

"All jokes aside a baby is a blessing. There is no such thing as a right time to have a baby. I know I joke a lot and shit, but I'm a man first. I got you and my seed for life."

"You promise?" I looked up and asked.

"Hell yeah. I told you months ago, I'd be a single father if it happened and you wasn't ready. For real I got you ma, stop crying. Let's go in here and feed my seed."

Chapter Seventeen

Kingston

Things between Burg and myself were going really good. If JuJu wasn't in the picture, she definitely has the potential to be a niggas mainline. I even took her by my folks' house to meet them. She clicked instantly with my moms. Hell, I think moms liked her more than she did MeMe and that said a lot because she loved the hell out of MeMe. I kinda felt bad about making her my side chic, but a nigga gotta do what a nigga gotta do. I had met most of her family a while back, but her moms and pops insisted a nigga come over so they can meet me in a different setting. I agreed and was glad her pops didn't come at a nigga with that don't hurt my baby bullshit like MeMe's dad did when I first met him.

That night after we left her parents, I asked her why her cousin Sascha didn't look like anybody in their family. Burg's mom had pulled out a bunch of old photo albums and Sascha stuck out in most of the pictures she was in.

"Sascha was adopted by my aunt and uncle when she was like four."

"That makes sense." I said as the wheels started turning in my head. The idea popped into my head again that Sascha, MeMe, and JuJu could be related. Shit, they all looked alike and they were adopted. Well not JuJu but still. Nah that shit only happens in the movies this is just a weird coincidence. I thought to myself.

That had been a few weeks ago and I was still having the what-if thoughts. I had just pulled up on JB because we had still been tryna put the play in motion with the connect but looks like we might have to change our plans. Every time I called the number Kwik gave me some dude always answered and told me he was gonna let the boss know and hung up.

"Sup, cuz?" JB walked up to my truck and asked as soon as I whipped in his yard.

"Shit I can't call it."

"Come on let's go in the house and figure this shit out."

"Bet." I got out and hit the locks on my door before following him into his crib.

"So, what we gonna do about this connect shit?"

"Man, I don't even know. I thought the shit was solid since it came from the nigga Kwik."

"Kwik? What Kwik? Nigga you ain't never mention nothing about the plug coming from no damn Kwik?"

"The fuck you mean Kwik? He was just some nigga I was locked up with. I ran it with him one day about my street dealings and he looked out with a plug for when I get out."

"Man, cuz I sure hope it ain't that lil crazy muhfucka Kwik that run with that nigga Banga."

"Shit, I don't know who he runs with, but why the fuck you over there looking all scared and shit?"

"You have been locked down for a minute cuz so you don't know shit about them niggas Kwik and Banga."

"Shit so you telling me you scared of these niggas or something?"

"I don't fear no man, but at the same time, I pick my battles wisely. If the Kwik you're talking about is the one I think it is, I suggest you fall back. Them niggas don't give a shit about nothing."

"Man, fuck that. I don't fear no nigga that bleeds just like me. I'll get this bread on my own since you scared." I told him walking out and slamming his door. I hopped in my car and sped off. JB's ass pissed me off. I needed to eat good and get my dick wet, so I called Burg.

"Hey, bae." She answered like she was happy to hear from a nigga.

"Sup, ma? What you up to?"

"Nothing much about to clock out and get out of here. What's up with you?"

"Shit, just leaving JB's house. You hungry, you wanna go out to eat?"

"I'm starving. I actually worked through lunch. What you got in mind?"

"I'll figure something out. I'm about to go home and change. I'll be there to pick you up at seven and crash with you after. How does that sound?"

"Perfect, I'll see you soon bae." She said before ending the call. I hopped on the interstate and headed home. I was pulling into my garage when my phone started ringing. I noticed it was JuJu calling and quickly answered the phone. I accepted the call, got out of the truck, and waited for it to connect.

"Sup, Ma?" I asked as soon as the call connected.

"Hey, boo? What you up to?"

"Shit just pulling up to the crib. How ya doing? Have you started counting down yet?"

"I'm good. Hell yeah. I've been crossing out the days on my calendar. Two more weeks and I'm free baby."

"I can't wait either. You ready to come home to daddy?"

"You know I am. I miss you so much."

"I told you I was gonna get you outta there."

"Yes, you did. Thank you so much for having my back. I could never repay you but I will damn sure try."

"You good Ma. I told ya I'm ya man and I got you."

"Well, bae I was just calling to hear your voice. I ain't gonna hold you I'm getting ready to hit the shower and watch a lil TV before I call it a night."

"Cool. I can't wait until you're in the shower with me."

"I know. It won't be long though. Talk to you later, Love you."

"Aight bae. Love you too." I said before ending the call. I went to my closet and grabbed me something to wear for my date with Burg tonight. I packed my overnight bag and then jumped in the shower. After I showered, I got dressed grabbed my bag, and went downstairs. I set the alarm before locking up and going to the garage to get in my truck. It was a quarter till seven when I pulled up to Burg's house.

Chapter Eighteen

Tyzir

I had been trying to find the right time to tell Yah about her siblings but something always came up when I did. We had our maternity shoot this morning with Sylozada Shots. The raw footage looked good as fuck so I already know the edited ones are gonna be even better. We were back at the house lounging around watching TV and figured I should tell her now.

"Hey, Yah can I talk to you about something?" I told her turning the TV off.

"Yeah, what's up?" She said as she sat up facing me.

"Before I start, I just want you to know it's strictly up to how you move forward with this information. I got ya back whatever you decide."

"Ummm ok I guess." She responded with a look of confusion on her face.

"You ever thought about it being strange that you ended up pregnant with triplets?"

"No, not really once the initial shock wore off, I just figured it was meant to be."

"Well to make a long story short, you're a triplet. You actually have a biological brother and a sister."

"Say what nah? I mean I knew I was adopted, but I never knew I had siblings let alone a triplet. How did you find this out?"

"Kingston."

"Oh, lordt please fill me in."

"I had a guy on the inside with him who kept us up-to-date just in case he ran off at the mouth and mentioned you are anything like that. He never mentioned you but he did get really close to his celly Julius Chavez but they call him JuJu."

"Ok, but what does that have to do with me having siblings?"

"I was getting to that before you cut me off."

"I didn't mean to interrupt you. I'm sorry this is so shocking but go ahead and finish the story."

"His celly is a tranny but hasn't fully transformed or however that shit goes. They think Kingston and JuJu might actually have had a sexual relationship."

"I KNOW YOU FUCKING LYING. You mean to tell me big bad Kingston is fucking a man?"

"Yeah, but there's more. I figured JuJu might be beneficial in case that nigga Kingston tried something when he got out so I had Pete look into him. That's how we found out JuJu is also your brother. He grew up in foster care but was never actually adopted. Your sister was born as Jalisa Chavez but her name was changed after she was adopted. Her name is Sascha Bradford and she lives in St. James Parish, in Grammercy I think, with her husband and her daughter."

"WOW. So, was my name changed too?"

"Yeah, it was actually changed from Janiya Chavez."

"So, Kingston smashed my brother in jail. I swear Baton Rouge is too small."

"Yeah, that's what they were saying, but he doesn't think the niggas in the dorm knew about it. Turns out he wrote JuJu a letter when he got out and some niggas in the dorm found it or some shit. They like a couple or something since he trying to get him out and move him in."

"Damn, this nigga is really gay. That's why he did me the way he did."

"Fuck that nigga. You forever good now. So, how do you feel about having siblings?"

"I thank God for you daily. Siblings, it's all so weird. I wonder if they look like me or if they even know about me. I would like to meet them but then there's the Kingston situation."

"I thank him twice daily for you Yah. I told you I'm with you no matter what you decide. From what I hear JuJu is wanting to find his biological relatives when he gets out, so this just may work out."

"Is JuJu still locked up?"

"Yes, he is but he's supposed to be getting out soon. What you got in mind Yah? I can see the wheels spinning in your head."

"Well, I was thinking that I can maybe go visit him? I know a prison is the last place I should be going big and pregnant but I feel it's the best way to avoid Kingston."

"Yeah, I really don't want you going to no prison. I'll allow you to go up there on one condition."

"What's that?"

"I'm going with you.

"Thanks, babe. Do you have any pictures of them and what about Sascha you have any information for her too?"

"I don't have any on hand but I know Pete can get it. I need to pull some strings to get us on JuJu's visiting list for the next visit. I have a few questions for him as well."

"What questions you got for him? You know what never mind. The less I know the better off I am."

"You catch on quick." I said laughing.

"Well now that we've gotten that outta the way, what do you wanna do the rest of the day?"

"You already know what I wanna do?" She replied with a smirk and crawled over to the edge of the bed. She sat up on the side with her feet dangling above the floor. "Come here." She motioned for me to come stand between her legs.

I already knew what time it was when she yanked my pants down and whipped my dick out in one motion. It had been a minute since I got some head but I ain't tripping. With her belly it's not always comfortable for her. A nigga ain't missing out on no pussy though. She has turned into a lil nympho. She grabbed my dick with one hand and eased it in her mouth sucking on it slowly like a Bomb Pop.

"Damn Yah."

She pulled it out and spit on it making it extra sloppy before she went in with no hands. I was hitting the back of her throat and she was taking that shit like a champ. Feeling my nut building up, I eased out of her mouth. Something about her swallowing while pregnant with my seeds just doesn't feel right to me. I gently picked her up and laid her on her side.

"You good bae?" I asked as I laid her gently on the side before laying behind her and sliding in her wetness. This is one of the most comfortable positions for her since we are limited on positions.

"Ooooooh babe. Right there, please don't stop." She screamed out as I long stroked her making sure to hit her spot each time. I sped up a little as I deepened my strokes.

"You want me to stop?"

"Fuck no. Whatever you do please don't stopppppppp." She moaned out really loud. "I'm about to cummmmmmmmm."

"Give it to me then, let it go."

"Aaaaahhhhhhhhhhhhhhh." She screamed as she came so hard her juices made a puddle. I delivered a few more stroked before I shot of my load. We laid in the same spot for a few moments before I got up to run her a bubble bath. Once I put her in the tub, I stripped the bed. I put a fresh set of bedding on the bed and took the others to the laundry room to wash.

"Wake up Yah." I gently shook her she had fallen asleep just that fast. Her eyes fluttered open and she licked her lips as she watched my dick hanging and swanging. "No ma'am. You already in her falling asleep. You'll get some more later. I'm sure you hungry by now, huh?"

"Yeah, I can definitely eat."

"What you got a taste for?"

"Hmm. I can really go for some spaghetti with pickles and ranch dressing on top.

"Yah that shit is gross. You and these weird-ass cravings. I'll cook after I shower though. Do you want something to eat for now?"

"Yeah, a peanut butter, pineapple, and pickle sandwich on cinnamon toast with a side of fruit."

"I got you, bae." I told her shaking my head. "Come on let me wash you up so you can go rinse off."

Chapter Nineteen

JuJu

I had been in good spirits ever since I got my release date. I literally have one week left and I would be outta here. I can't wait to get home to my man. I was chilling in my cell listening to the music when the guard came got me for a visit.

"Visit? Is it my lawyer?" I asked confused since I have never got any visits besides Renzetti.

"Look man, I don't have time for twenty-one questions. Either you come to the visit or I can tell them you refused." The fat ass guard said with attitude. I hopped up and made sure my appearance was straight before walking over to him to get cuffed.

He led me to the visitor's room, uncuffed my wrists and I just stood there confused. I looked around for any familiar faces and I didn't see anyone I knew. I looked around and noticed a man and woman sitting at a table. Something about the lady looked familiar, but I couldn't put my finger on it. They looked my way and waved me over. I looked behind me to make sure they were talking to me. Since there was no one behind me, I slowly walked towards them. I made it over to the table and stood there quietly.

"Julius?" The guy spoke up first.

"Yea but I prefer JuJu and you are?"

"I'm TC and this is my wife MeMe. Why don't you have a seat." I sat across from them. The woman I now knew as MeMe still hadn't said anything but she just stared at me. "I know you're probably wondering why we are here so let's get down to business."

"Hi, JuJu." MeMe finally spoke up and smiled at me. "I'm your sister."

"Sister? What are you talking about?" I asked wanting to hear more.

"I recently found out about you due to your connection to my ex."

"Your ex. Who's your ex and how is he connected to me?" I sat straight up and asked.

"Kingston Francois." She replied with a raised eyebrow.

"Oh Killa K. I don't really know much about him he was just my cellmate before he got released."

"Look man you don't have to downplay it to us. We already know what's up." TC interrupted.

"I don't know what you guys are implying, but what makes you think we're sisters?" I asked MeMe avoiding eye contact with TC. Everything about this nigga screams BOSS and I don't want to problems with him. I guess that's why she looked familiar to me, shit we look alike.

"Well, it's a little deeper than just being siblings. We're actually two thirds of a set of triplets. We have a sister who I haven't met yet. I wanted to meet you first before you were released."

"How did you know I was getting released?"

"TC pulled some strings. Do you know why Kingston was in prison?"

"No, not really. Whenever I asked, he would brush it off and say he got railroaded on some bullshit."

"Let's just say he basically beat me and left me for dead. He was pouring gas around my house and was about to set it on fire until my neighbor caught him in the act." My mouth fell open in shock.

"Oh my God, are you serious?" I just had to ask but I knew she wasn't lying. I could see it in her eyes everything she was saying was the truth.

"There's more, a few months ago he kidnapped me. Thank God TC found me in time and got me away before he came back. I know this is a lot to take in, but I would like to get to know you."

"You're right this is a lot. The funny thing is I planned to start digging and find my biological family when I get out of here. And look at God you showed up here today."

"Whew. I wasn't sure how you would feel after I told you about that monster Kingston.

Whatever you do, please don't ever mention me to him or that you even met me."

"I can definitely do that. I am supposed to move in with him when I get out but after all this info you just dropped, I may need to rethink my plans."

"If you back out, he may get suspicious and wanna know why. So, you gotta move smart, and whatever you do, don't ever let your guard down around him. Here's my number."

She discreetly slid me a folded piece of paper with her name and number.

"If you need anything once you're out please don't hesitate to call me. Well, time is up so we better get going." They both stood up and I did as well.

"It was nice meeting you both." I said as I stuck my hand out for them to shake. TC shook my hand, MeMe walked around TC to hug me and that's when I noticed her huge baby bump. "OMG, you're pregnant sis? What are you having?"

"Yes, I am. Triplets. Two boys and a girl." She said with a huge smile.

"Congratulations guys. To answer your question, I would love to get to know you and I've made up my mind to get away from Kingston as quickly as possible. I don't have any family but I would love to build one with you." I told her honestly.

"We'll talk." She winked at me as they got ready to leave. "See, you on the outside." She said as the guard led me away.

I was floating on cloud nine walking back to my dorm. I have not one but two sisters. I wonder what my other sister is like, I thought to myself. That shit about Killa K really left a bad taste in my mouth. He not only tried to kill my sister, but got his ass out of jail and kidnapped her while she's pregnant. That made me wonder what else he might have been out there doing. I'm still going to stay with him, but the game has definitely changed.

Once I was back in my cell, I unfolded the paper MeMe had slipped me. It had her number and the name Janiya on it. I copied the name and number on my notepad of important numbers before tossing the paper in the trash.

Chapter Twenty

Mareyah

"So, what are you gonna do about Cardell?" I asked Monique as we sat in my backyard eating the boiled seafood from Fiery Crab she brought. She was off today and wanted to come chill with me.

"Shit, I've been following his ass for damn near two weeks and he hasn't even noticed. I've seen enough to know the nigga on that shit. I mean do I just come out and ask him if he is smoking crack or do I wait until I come home and realize he done smoked up my muthafuckin TVs and shit?" She said with a straight face as I fell out laughing. "MeMe this shit ain't funny."

"My bad. I'm not laughing at the situation but how you said it. All jokes aside I think you just need to sit down and talk to him. When you're talking to him, don't make him feel like you're judging him. You have to be sincere in your approach otherwise he's not gonna tell you anything and most likely start avoiding you."

"I don't know, I think he might get offended and flash out. What if I do like they do on TV and set up an intervention?"

"That might not be a good idea. An intervention might be just a little premature in this case. I still say just try talking to him and ask him if anything is going on or if there is something that he needs to tell you?"

"As his wife, I gotta figure it out soon and try to get him some help. Enough about that, you ready for your baby shower?"

"Yessssss. I can't wait to see how over the top y'all went."

"Girl once we decided on a theme Auntie Erycka went crazy. I can't wait to see how it all comes together though. Have y'all decided on any names yet?"

"Oh Lordt. I can only imagine, you know my mama extra as fuck. We have a couple of names, but we haven't narrowed it down yet. We're not telling anyone the names until I deliver."

"Bitch I already figured the babies names would be a secret. So, have you heard from JuJu since he got out?"

"I've talked to him once. He called to let me know he was out and safe. He's staying with Kingston until he can figure things out and get away from him."

"Damn. This shit is so crazy. Kingston's gay and fucking your brother. I always knew he was a pussy, but damn I didn't know he liked boy pussy. Did you ever get the chance to meet your sister?"

"No, not yet but I plan to do that soon. I got too much going on and not enough time to do it. I'll try to get around to it next week though."

"You ain't lying. Y'all got event after event and I love it. So, bitch you ready to be Mrs. Tyzir Muthafuckin Cunard?"

"Hell yeah. I can't wait. Thursday isn't getting here fast enough."

"And ain't. Well, the girls and I are coming by Wednesday after work. You know we can't let you get married without throwing you a bachelorette party."

"Awww. Y'all don't have to do that."

"Bitch whet? We've already ordered the food and got the drinks on deck, well virgin drinks on deck for your ass." We sat outside laughing and talking until we were done eating. We cleaned up our mess, washed our hands before going back into the house. "That's a damn shame." She said as I yawned.

"Shut up heaux. These babies take all my lil energy. I need a nap now shit."

"Well come on, I'll help you upstairs so you can shower and get in the bed before I leave."

"Girl I'll be fine you don't have to stay."

"Whatever bitch. I'm not in a rush to go home anyway." After my shower, I threw on one of TC's t-shirts and climbed into the bed. Once Nique made sure I was good, she left. It didn't take long for me to fall asleep.

I woke up to the sound of the shower running and sat up in bed. I grabbed my phone and saw that it was a little after seven-thirty. *Damn, I must've really been tired*, I thought as I got up to go pee. I wobbled in the bathroom and sat down on the toilet to relieve my bladder while watching TC through the glass of the shower door. I kinda felt like a perv with my mouth watering sitting there watching him as he soaped up his dick. I wiped myself quickly before jumping up and snatching the t-shirt over my head and wobbled my ass to the shower.

"I'm surprised it took you so long."

"Huh, what are you talking about?" I feigned ignorance as I bit my lip to camouflage my smile. I swear this pregnancy has me hornier than a two-dicked Billy goat.

"I heard you when you came in here. I was watching you watch me." He said as he pulled me closer to him. He gently grabbed me by my throat, slowly tilting my head back before slipping his tongue in my mouth. In one quick motion, he had me bent over the bench. I grabbed ahold of the bench seat to make sure I didn't fall as he slowly entered my dripping wet pussy.

"Oooooooohhhhh shitttttt." I moaned out as I threw it back at him. This belly ain't stopping nothing. TC was balls deep and the only thing that could be heard was my moaning, his grunting, and our skin slapping against each other.

He wrapped his hands around my ponytail pulling my head back while he continued to hit me with long, deep strokes. I felt my eyes rolling in the back of my head. My breath got caught in my throat preventing me from being able to announce I was cumming as my juices swiftly ran down my thighs.

"I'm bout to cum Yah." He yelled out before hitting me with a few more strokes before filling me up and pulling out. "That shit is lethal." He said as he slapped me on my ass. I tried to stand up, but my legs felt like noodles and I almost fell. He quickly picked me up and sat me on the bench before I bust my ass. TC washed me up and once I felt like I could stand, I rinsed off before getting out of the shower. He got out right after, wrapped a towel around his waist, and helped me apply my body butter before helping me into my nightshirt.

I sat on the bed thinking impure thoughts as I watch him slip on his boxers and pajama pants.

"You wanna come downstairs and eat?" He asked.

"Hell yeah. What'd you bring me?"

"Nothing, I made you grilled chicken breast, roasted potatoes, and broccoli with cheese when I came in from work."

"I bet you did." I mumbled while rolling my eyes unenthused since he had been on me about my eating habits after my last doctor's appointment. Dr. Henderson mentioned my blood pressure being slightly higher than normal and my glucose numbers indicated I was borderline for gestational diabetes.

"Don't act like that bae. I just wanna make sure you and my seeds are good before you end up in the hospital for being hardheaded."

"I know babe, I'm just so used to eating what I want with no consequences. I just don't wanna be walking around here on pins and needles about what to eat and what not to eat."

"You don't have to be on pins and needles bae, just be mindful of what you're eating and how it can affect you." He told me as he kissed me on the lips before helping me up, so we can go downstairs. I took a seat at the island while he fixed our plates.

"Babe, when you're free do you think you can take me to meet Sascha?"

"Sure, we can go tomorrow if you want."

"It's no rush but whatever works for you. I feel like I put it off long enough. I wonder if everything is ok with JuJu. I haven't heard from him since he got out."

"It's cool. I don't have anything really planned for tomorrow. Hopefully, everything is everything with him. I'm sure if something was wrong, he knows he can call us."

"Thanks, babe. I wasn't sure how you felt knowing his connection to Kingston."

"That's your blood so I'm cool with him unless he shows me he is on bullshit." He said, placing my plate down in front of me and sitting his down across from me before going get our drinks.

"I wanted to invite him to the baby shower, but wasn't sure if it would be a good idea or not."

"I'm cool with it if that's what you wanna do, we'll just have to take precautions to make sure you're safe."

"This chicken is bomb babe." I said being honest and forgetting that the shit was supposed to be healthy. We sat around eating and suddenly I got a weird feeling. I tried to shake the feeling and continued to eat my food.

"What's wrong Yah?"

"Nothing, why you ask?"

"Lie to me again. I know you better than you know yourself, so what's up?"

"Honestly, I don't know. I just got a feeling something bad is gonna happen."

"It's probably just your nerves. You know I'ma do whatever I can to make sure you straight."

"I know babe and that's why I love you."

Chapter Twenty-One

Kingston

I thought I would be able to handle this shit with Burg and JuJu being home, but a nigga was stressed the fuck out. I'm used to coming and going as I pleased. This getting interrogated every time I walk through the door is new to me. JuJu ain't popped a nigga off with no ass since she been out but have the audacity to question a nigga about where I've been and what I'm doing. I'm trying to be understanding because she suffers from PTSD after being raped but this shit is getting old and fast.

Burg ain't making it no better either, cause she constantly nagging me about why I haven't been sleeping over and shit. A nigga running out of lies like Johnnie Taylor. It's three o'clock in the damn morning and I'm just leaving Burg's house. She wouldn't let a nigga leave so to keep the peace, I pretended I was staying the night and waited until she fell asleep to sneak out. I kinda felt bad about leaving shorty's crib like that. At least I remembered to set the alarm before I left. I hope JuJu is in bed sleep because I don't feel like arguing with her ass tonight. It didn't take me long to get home since there weren't many cars on the road.

I pulled my truck in the garage, got out, and tried quietly to ease my way into the house. I locked the door and passed by the living room getting ready to walk up the stairs when the light flipped on.

"Fuck." I said turning around to face JuJu. I could tell by her facial expression she was pissed.

"Look who finally found their way home." She said sarcastically and rolled her eyes.

"Man, bae don't start that shit tonight. A nigga been grinding all day and I just wanna shower and get some sleep."

"Grinding all day huh? Let me smell ya dick then."

"Get the fuck outta here with that dumb shit." I told her as I turned back around and started walking up the stairs. She must've flown across the room because when I looked back, she was on my heels coming up the stairs, talking shit, and clapping her hands. Instead of arguing with her, I continued to make my way to the bathroom. I started the shower while I stripped outta my clothes, I pulled my pants off and shit hit the fan.

"Nigga where the fuck is your draws?" She asked in a voice so calm I got scared.

"Bae it ain't what it looks like," I tried to explain as she went crazy and started swinging on me. I tried my best to get her off of me without putting my hands on her, but the bitch wouldn't stop swinging. Her licks was connecting and they were hard as a bitch. I can't lie JuJu throw them bitches like a nigga. I have never had a woman hit me as hard as she was and before I knew it, I had two-pieced her ass. I instantly felt bad, but I had to do something to get her off of me.

"Say ma, get up." I bent down shaking her awake. "Come on bae get up, I apologize."

She wasn't responding, so rolled her over and that's when I saw blood. I looked closer and noticed the gash on her head. I stood up confused because I know damn well I didn't hit her that fucking hard. I looked around and saw the blood on the counter and realized she must've hit her head when she fell. I had to get her to a hospital but I couldn't call 911. A nigga ain't tryna go back to jail. I started to panic as I paced back and forth trying to figure out what to do then it hit me, I can drop her off in front of the hospital. That way I can get her some medical attention without getting my ass into any trouble.

I grabbed a towel, scooped up her phone, and threw it in her purse. I ran downstairs to my truck, I spread the towel across the seat to catch the blood, tossed her purse on the floor, and started the truck. I ran back upstairs and picked her up off the floor and quickly carried her back down to the truck. I laid her on the seat before going to the driver's side. Once the garage was open, I did the dash to the nearest hospital. About six minutes later, I was pulling up to Prairieville Family Hospital. I threw my shit in park, reached over to open the door, and gently pushed her out. I grabbed her purse, tossed it out on side of her, slammed the door, and drove the fuck off. I went back home to clean up the mess, shower, and lay my ass down.

I got in bed and stared at the ceiling paranoid as fuck. I prayed JuJu would be ok and prayed even harder that the cops didn't come knocking on my door. My phone started ringing instantly causing my mind to race even more. I let out a breath of relief when I saw Burg's name flashing across the screen.

"Sup, Ma?" I answered the phone trying to sound calm.

"Where are you?"

"Home."

"Home. Really Kingston, is there somebody else?"

"No, bae. Don't start that bullshit. A nigga had some business to handle and I ended up coming home after I finished."

"Since, when do you have a business to handle in the middle of the night? I call bullshit."

"I'm serious, I was handling business. You know when the money calls I gotta answer."

"Yeah, whatever. Well since you at home, I'm on my way." She said as she sounded like she was moving around getting dressed.

"No." I yelled out a little louder than I intended to.

"What the hell you mean no?"

"I didn't mean it like that. I just don't want you out driving at this hour the shit ain't safe. How bout I just come back over. Will that make you feel better?"

"Yeah whatever, you just better not take too long to get here. I don't know what you got going on all of a sudden but you better not let me find out." She said ending the call.

I got up and grabbed my duffle bag and threw some shit in it to hold me for a few days in case I needed to hide out and her crib. Once I had everything, I needed I made my way downstairs, set the alarm, locked up, and got in my truck to head back to Burg's house.

Chapter Twenty-Two

Banga

Shira has really been testing a nigga lately, but it's time I showed her just who the fuck I am. Every time I ask if she has made a decision about moving in with me, all she says is she is still thinking. I told her out the gate if she took too long, that I would decide for her and I've made my decision. We went to her doctor's appointment the other day and they confirmed she's ten weeks pregnant. She's pregnant with my seed and that's reason enough for her to move in with me, but since she wanna be difficult I'ma handle the shit. I'm headed to her crib right now to meet the moving company I hired. I don't just lay the dick down, I lay down the law too and she gon' learn that shit today.

I pulled up, grabbed the boxes off the passenger seat, and made my way inside to pack up her personal stuff like her panties, bras, toys, and stuff I didn't want the movers touching. I had been packing for about thirty minutes when the doorbell rang. I knew it was most likely the movers so I went to let them in.

"Sup, bruh?" I opened the door.

"Hello, Mr. Montgomery. I'm Dave with All My Sons Moving and I just need to get your signature here, here, and here." He told me as he passed me the clipboard.

"Here ya go, bruh," I signed, passed it back to him, and stepped aside to let them in so they can get to work.

"Is there any particular area you want us to start?" Dave asked looking around the room.

"Yeah, y'all can start in the front and work y'all way to the back. I should be finished in the bedroom and outta y'all way by then."

"Sounds like a plan." It took me about an hour to finish what I was doing. I grabbed the boxes and took them to my truck. I walked to the front they had cleared out the entire kitchen and dining room. These niggas move fast as fuck and was just about finished with the living room. I looked at my watch to check the time and figured we would be finished way ahead of schedule. I'd be home unpacking this shit by the time she comes home from work and see the decision I made.

It was a quarter until four by the time the movers and I were headed to my house to unload the boxes. I didn't think this shit through as far as where all of this shit was gonna go, but I'll figure that out later. Once we made it to my house, I gave them directions on what will go in the house, the garage, and the storage room in the back. My phone rang and I already knew it was Baby Mama without even looking at it.

"Sup, baby mama."

"Bae, I just got home from work, and somebody done broke in and took everything." I had to mute the phone to laugh. I know damn well she didn't really believe someone broke in. Lord, please don't let my baby mama be secretly slow.

"I'm at home, lock up and come straight here so we can figure this shit out."

"Come over there for what? Nigga are you not listening? Somebody done stole all my shit." She yelled through the phone.

"Ain't nobody stole shit. I told ya ass if you took too long or chose wrong, I would decide for ya and that's what I did."

"Are you fucking INSANE?"

"Look calm yo ass down before you upset my baby. I'll see you when you get home." I hung up on her ass. I didn't have time to be going back and forth with her over nonsense. She has no choice but to get with the program. I put my phone back in my pocket and focused back on the movers and making sure everything was being put where I told them to. About five minutes later my phone was ringing again, this time it was TC.

"Sup, bruh?" I answered as I stood off to the side observing.

"Bruh, please tell me you didn't really go through with that shit?"

"Baby mama must've called sis and told her I done cleared the crib out."

"Foo, I didn't think you were serious when you mentioned that shit to me the other day. She done called Yah all upset and crying and now Yah ass is pissed at you and shit."

"Tell sis her friend is hardheaded and will soon learn to follow her man's lead."

"Bruh, so you just gone force her to live with you against her will?"

"My mind was made up when I asked her to move in, I just wanted to make her feel like she had some input in the shit. Between me and you, she's pregnant with my seed and that just sealed the deal."

"Word? Congratulations bruh. That's what's up our babies are gonna grow up together like us."

"You already know. Please don't tell MeMe though. Baby mama told me not to tell anybody and I don't wanna hear her mouth about the shit."

"Say less bruh. Let me go in here and calm Yah ass down. I'll get up with you later. One L."

"One L." I said ending the call shaking my head. I see I'ma have to teach baby mama about putting folks in our mix. Gotta nip that shit in that bud before she starts thinking that shit is cool.

The movers had unloaded everything and were now gone. I was upstairs in the bedroom unpacking boxes and shit. I was hanging her clothes in the closet when I heard the front door slam. I stopped what I was doing and went downstairs to deal with her ass."

"Sup, baby mama." I told her when I made it to the bottom of the stairs where she was standing with a mug on her face.

"Why did you move my things without my permission?"

"Did you not just hear me speak to you? It was rude of you not to speak back." I told her as she rolled her eyes.

"Hey, Banga." She said with an attitude.

"Since I'm Banga, I take it you're mad. Come on upstairs so you can get the shit off your chest." I said stepping to the side so I can follow her up. Once upstairs I went to the bathroom and ran her a bubble bath and poured in some of those essential oils she loves. I came back and she was still standing in the same spot with her hands folded.

"Fix ya face." I told her as I unfolded her hands and began to undress her.

"I don't get how you are just moving around like I'm not supposed to be mad about what you did. Are you just gonna disregard my feelings?" I bent down and lifted her legs one by one to remove her shoes and helped her step outta her skirt that had fallen around her ankles when I unzipped it.

"Shhhh, stop fussing before you stress my baby out."

"Ooooh." She moaned as I pulled her panties down with my teeth and blew on her clit before continuing to pull them off. I stood back up and unhooked her bra and grabbed her hand leading her to the bathroom. I helped her in the tub and sat on the side ready to get this conversation over with.

"Check it. I know you pissed at a nigga and shit but a nigga tired of going back and forth between both cribs. Shit, a nigga got more than enough space and I done got used to having you around. You pregnant with my seed and I want us all under the same roof."

"I get that, but I feel powerless in this whole situation and if I allow you to get away with this then, you'll feel like you can control me and that would be another problem altogether."

"I'm not tryna control you at all. I love the fact that you're independent and have a backbone. As your man and father of your child, all I ask is that you let me do me and lead the way. I'm nothing like them other suckas you used to, but I can't prove that to you when you fighting me on everything. Yeah, this shit is all new to me, but I wouldn't wanna do it with anyone else. Shit, a nigga love your ass even more now that you carrying my son."

"I hear you but actions speak louder than words. Everything you're saying sounds good and all- Wait did you say you love me?"

"Seriously, you can't tell? I've been showing you that for months. You are something else. Look I'll make a deal with you, let's trying living together for thirty days and we'll revisit the subject. Once the thirty days are up if you don't wanna stay, I'll call the moving company and have them move all of your stuff back to ya crib. Deal?"

"I guess it's a deal. I love you too Osiris." She said smiling for the first time since she's been here."

"Girl bye. You don't love me, you just love the way I write my name in that pussy." I told her as she splashed water on me. I got up leaving her alone and went back to putting her clothes and shoes in the closet.

Chapter Twenty-Three

Tyzir

I agreed to take YahYah to Grammercy today to meet her sister for the first time. Hopefully, she's home and doesn't feel some type of way about us showing up unannounced. I gave her the same speech I did before going to meet JuJu. I told her not to go in with the assumption that Sascha will automatically be receptive to her.

After meeting JuJu, she had so many questions for her folks but they just didn't have any answers. They were just as shocked as she was to find out she was a triplet. They said they were never given any inclination she had siblings let alone being a triplet otherwise they would've adopted all three to keep them together.

"Hey, bae you ready to hit the highway?" I asked walking into the room as she slid her feet in Tory Burch sandals. I had to readjust my dick after looking at how good she looked in the cute lil maternity sundress she was wearing. Pregnancy definitely looked good as fuck on her, belly and all.

"Yeah, let me just grab my bag and I'm ready." I helped her down the stairs and she flew into the kitchen once she had caught her breath. I laughed already knowing she was going to get a snack to hold her until lunchtime. Once she had everything she needed we were on our way.

"Are you nervous about meeting Sascha?"

"Yes and no. I mean what if she doesn't believe me or want to have anything to do with me."

"Think positive bae. We'll cross that bridge if we even we have to cross it." I told her grabbing her hand and squeezing it gently before bringing it up to my mouth to kiss it."

"Yeah, I guess you're right babe. This is all so weird like a scene out of a ghetto soap opera or something. I wonder how JuJu is doing. I'll call and check up on him later on. You never said anything but how do you feel about JuJu being transgender?"

"Shit, I don't feel anything. That's his lifestyle. I'm secure in my manhood enough to respect other people's sexual orientation and/or preferences. As long as he doesn't come at me on no sideways shit and disrespect me or you, we good."

"You're the best babe. I just didn't know if you being around her makes you uncomfortable or something."

"Uncomfortable? Why would I be uncomfortable? I'm a man bae. The ones that be uncomfortable are them down low ass niggas who keep getting caught with em."

"I guess that makes sense but you are gonna have to use her preferred pronouns. It's disrespectful to say he and him when he identifies as a woman."

"I can dig it. Respect goes both ways so I'll have to get in the habit of saying the correct thing."

"I'm starting to get used to it. JuJu and I resemble each other, but I wonder if Sascha and I look more alike."

"Well, you'll soon find out. According to the GPS, we'll be pulling up in about four minutes." She flipped down the visor, checking her appearance and reapplying her lip gloss. "You look beautiful as usual bae." I told her causing her to turn red from blushing. A few minutes later we were pulling in the driveway of what appeared to be the biggest house on the street. "You ready to do this bae?"

"As ready as I'll ever be." She looked over at me and nervously said. I shut off the car, got out, and went around to help her out. We walked up the few steps on the porch and rang the doorbell.

"Relax Yah." I told her rubbing her back trying to help calm her nerves.

"Who is it?" A voiced on the other side of the door asked.

"Hi my name is Mareyah and I have my fiancé Tyzir with me. I just have some information for you." Yah said as the door slowly opened.

"How can I help you?" The lady asked as we stood there in shock. She looked identical to

Yah. I guess she was in shock too because she and Yah were just staring at each other. For them, it was probably like looking in a damn mirror.

"I'm assuming just by everyone's reaction, you're Sascha." I spoke up first. "I'm Tyzir but everyone calls me TC and this is my fiancée Mareyah. Due to some recent unfortunate events, we discovered that you guys are siblings, well actually triplets. Do you mind if we come in and talk to you for a few minutes?"

"Yes, yes please come in." She stepped aside and led us into her den. "Can I get you guys anything?"

"No thank you. We're good." I told her since Yah still hadn't found her voice.

"This is the weirdest thing that has ever happened to me. We have each other's entire face. Oh my God, you're pregnant. Congratulations. How far along are you? I have so many questions let me shut up so you can talk." She said genuinely excited.

"Yes, I'm currently twenty-four weeks pregnant with triplets. Two boys, and a girl."

"Oh, wow that is awesome. Are these your first? I have a six-year-old daughter named Sa'Irah."

"Thank you, yes these are our first. That's a beautiful name."

"Thank you, she should be waking up from her nap soon and you can meet her. So, we're triplets, do we have a sister or brother?"

"We have a sister named JuJu, well technically she was born our brother Julius; however, she's trans and identifies as a woman. She actually favors us as well. I found out about both of you after my ex-boyfriend Kingston kidnapped me a few months ago. He was recently released from prison and turns out he and JuJu became a couple while they were doing time together."

"Wait you taking me too fast. Say what nah? Our trans sister was dating your ex-boyfriend while they were in jail. This is some real-life reality TV shit. Thank God you are ok. Where is Kingston now? Is he back in jail."

"No, not at the moment. JuJu got out not too long ago and moved in with him. I told him if he changed his mind and backed out of staying with him, then Kingston would have questions."

"Oh, so they're a couple couple. I guess Kingston is a popular name these days. I met one not too long ago. My lil cousin has a new boyfriend named Kingston that she brought over." I looked at Yah and could tell what she was thinking by her facial expression.

"Sascha I could already tell what my baby is thinking. If we don't know anything else, we know Baton Rouge is too damn small. Do you remember how your cousin's boyfriend Kingston looked?"

"I can do better he's on some of the pictures we took. Give me one sec to go grab them." I'll be right back.

"I got a strange feeling it's gonna be him, babe." Yah whispered to me.

"Yeah, bae I got that same feeling. Hopefully, it's not."

"Hey, guys look who's awake. Sa'Irah say hi to our guests, this is your Uncle TC and your Aunt Mareyah."

"Hey." She shyly waved at me ran full speed towards Yah. She hugged her as tight as Yah's belly would allow. She looked like a mini replica of Sascha and Yah with a head full of curly hair.

"Oh, she really likes you. She has never warmed up to anybody as fast as she has to you."

"Mommy, she has your face." Sa'Irah's lil squeaky voice said looking back and forth between Sascha and Yah.

"Yes, she does. Isn't she beautiful?" Sa'Irah nodded her head.

"Is this him?" She asked pointing him out in the pics she held in front of us.

"Unfortunately, that's definitely him." YahYah responded after looking at the first picture.

"Listen I know you don't know us from a can of paint, but please take what I'm about to say as seriously as possible. He is a monster and is very dangerous. He was in jail for beating Yah and attempting to set her house on fire. Then he snatched her up while she's pregnant. luckily we found her when we did. Lastly, you need to warn your cousin. He's not only a psycho but he's clearly living a double life."

"Oh my God. This is too much."

"Whatever you do when talking to your cousin don't mention my name or my nickname MeMe. It may be best to use my birthname Janiya if you need to when talking to her, just in case he is around."

"Janiya, so what your name was changed?"

"Yeah, my adopted parents changed my name when I was a baby."

"So, wait, you're Janiya, there's Julius, and I guess I'm Jalisa huh?"

"Yeah, how did you know that? I have memories of being called that name up until I started living with my adopted parents, then they started calling be Sascha."

"Our whole adoption process was weird. My parents didn't even know I was a triplet and poor JuJu was never adopted."

"Oh no poor him. I mean her, that's awful. I can't wait to meet her and hopefully bond with the both of you, if that's ok?"

"I would love that." Yah said smiling. "Well sorry to unload all of this on you at once but we need to be going, we have a few errands to run."

"Oh no, it's quite alright. It was a pleasure to meet you both and learning a few new things about me. I can't wait till my husband gets home so I can blow his mind."

"Well, here's my number. Please don't hesitate to call me. My baby shower is coming up soon and I would love for you to come."

"Girl I will definitely be putting your number to use. Yes, I would love that."

"I have your address and I will make sure to send you an invitation." We all stood up and gave each other hug.

"Byeeeee." Sa'Irah said with a smile.

"It was a pleasure meeting you both. Don't be a stranger," Sascha said walking us to the door."

"Talk to you soon. Bye Sa'Irah." Yah said as I helped her down the steps and to the car. Once I was behind the wheel, I headed back to Baton Rouge to get Yah to her hair appointment.

Chapter Twenty-Four

JuJu

I woke up the next morning with a banging ass headache and the sounds of machines beeping around me. I slowly tried to open my eyes to see where the beeping sound was coming from, but the light was too bright and making my head hurt even more. I used my arm as a shield blocking some of the light as I once again opened my eyes.

"Ah look who's finally up." A sweet voice I didn't recognize said.

"Where am I?" I asked sitting up in bed.

"You're at Prairieville Family Hospital. I'm your day shift nurse and my name is Lori. Are you currently feeling any pain?"

"Hospital? How did I get here? My head is killing me."

"Awww sweetie. Unfortunately, you were found lying in front of the emergency room entrance last night. On a scale of 1-10 with ten being the worse, how would you rate your pain?"

"About a seven."

"I'll be right back to let the doctor know you're awake. I'll bring you something back for pain too."

"Thank you." I said as I began to wonder how I ended up in front of the hospital. I tried to replay the events from last night in my head. I remember sitting in the living room drinking a bottle of wine waiting on Killa K to get home. There was a knock on the door interrupting my thoughts.

"Hello, Sir." A voice said and I looked towards the door where it was coming from.

"Hi, it's ma'am." I said correcting him.

"Sorry about that. I am Dr. Leblanc. We were able to stitch that cut in your head and it may leave a small scar. You also have a mild concussion that I want to continue to monitor overnight. Do you have any questions for me?"

"That's ok. Thank you. I don't have any questions at the moment."

"Hello, do you mind if we ask a few questions?" One of two Ascension Parish Sheriff's officers asked.

"What kind of questions?"

"I'm Corporal Landry and this is Deputy Arceneaux. We just have some questions regarding last night. Do you have a few minutes?"

"I'm not sure if I can be of any help. I've been trying to remember what happened myself and can't really remember anything beyond drinking wine waiting on my boyfriend to come home."

"Boyfriend? What's your boyfriend's name? Where do you live? Has he contacted you or been here to visit?" Corporal Landry asked and I panicked because I didn't know if I should provide Killa K's information, but at the same time I don't know if he's safe or not. I would feel bad if something happened to him and I withheld information that could help.

"His name is Kingston Francois and our address is 14086 Airline Hwy. Our building number is twenty-three and our apartment number is 1423.

I'm unsure if he has been here or not, but I also don't know if he's in any danger."

"What kind of vehicle does he drive?" Deputy Arceneaux asked, speaking for the first time.

"A red Maserati SUV." I said noticing how they both looked at each other.

"Based on surveillance footage, you were pushed out of a red Maserati SUV last night. The driver tossed your purse out beside you and before speeding off."

"Do you recall getting in Mr. Francois's vehicle last night?"

"No, I don't. I just don't think he would do something like that to me. Is it possible that it was a vehicle like his or maybe someone attacked us and stole his truck?" I asked not wanting to believe he did what they are saying even with his history with my sister.

"Well, we got a partial image of the license plate that we're running which will help us determine if it was his vehicle or not. In the meantime, we're gonna go by the house and see if we can question him." Arceneaux stated after writing in his notepad.

"We're gonna release the surveillance footage to the public in hopes we get some leads. Here's my card, please contact me if you think of anything no matter how small it is every single detail counts. You take care." Leblanc said passing me his card.

"Thank you both."

"Here you go, baby. I brought you some crackers and pain meds in case you need something on your stomach to take it. If you're hungry, here's the information to order you some food." Nurse Lori said standing next to me as she passed the crackers, medication, and a lil cup of water to me.

"Thank you so much, ma'am. I'll just eat the crackers for now and order something when I wake up from my nap. Do you happen to know where my purse is?" I asked her just before she made it to the door to leave.

"Yes, I put it away for you. It's right over here, I'll grab it." She said as she went to the closet and grabbed my purse. "Do you need anything else?"

"No ma'am I'll be ok for now. Thank you again."

"Try to get some rest. I'll be back to check on you." She said before leaving and closing the door behind her.

The first thing I did was check my purse to make sure everything was still there. I didn't see anything missing so I grabbed my phone. I only had about thirty percent battery life so I didn't wanna do to much since I don't have my charger with me. I scrolled through my call log to see if Killa K had tried to contact him but the only thing I saw was all of the unanswered calls I made to him last night. The last outgoing call I made was at three thirty-nine am. I checked the text messages and pretty much had the same results. I tossed the phone back in my purse, putting my purse in between my legs, so it wouldn't get stolen if someone came in while I slept. After getting comfortable in bed, I drifted off to sleep.

It was a little after two in the afternoon when I woke up and my head was no longer pounding. My stomach growled reminding me to go ahead and call in my food order. I got up to go to the bathroom, after emptying my bladder I grabbed the face towel and washed my face. I went got back in bed once I was done and turned the TV on. I flipped through the channels and ended up stopping on the noon news replay. I was digging in my purse when I heard, "*a transgender woman was dumped in front of a Prairieville Hospital and authorities need your help identifying the driver of this vehicle. Please contact the Ascension Parish Crime Stoppers at 225-647-STOP with any information. All calls remain anonymous and you could be eligible for a tip.*"

I sat watching the clip of me being pushed out of the car followed by my purse being tossed out and the car speeding off. The partial license plate confirmed it was definitely Killa K's truck. I had seen it enough to know. The video must've triggered something because I suddenly started to remember the rest of the previous night's event. I remembered sitting in the dark waiting to confront him when he so-called tried to sneak into the house. I had followed him upstairs going off while he got undressed to get in the shower. He ain't have on no fucking draws, I flashed out and started swinging before he hit me back and everything went black.

Chapter Twenty-Five

Mareyah

TC and I left Sascha's house and were heading to my hair appointment with my girl Keisha at BeautifulMe Studio. I had to get my hair done today since we're getting married tomorrow morning.

"Babe, what do you think about Sascha?" I asked as we were riding on the interstate.

"She seemed pretty cool. I think it's crazy how much y'all look alike. Y'all gotta be identical and were in the same sac or however it goes."

"I swear when she opened that door, I was speechless. I felt like I was literally looking at myself in the mirror."

"Shit Yah, I think we were all speechless. Her daughter looks like y'all too. Her little facial expression was hilarious when she kept looking back at forth at y'all."

"Yeah, she's so pretty. I can't believe I have a niece. I wonder if our baby girl will look like her."

"She is adorable. It's crazy how Kingston's dumb ass reunited a family that had no clue the other even existed. Seeing how strong y'all genes are I would be surprised if she didn't." He said laughing.

"I definitely didn't expect her to drop that bomb about her lil cousin dating him. Is Baton Rouge really that small?"

"That shit is beyond weird. I know damn well he must've had some questions for Sascha at least when he first met her."

"Right hell I would have had twenty-one questions or more. I almost had a few questions myself." I said as we were pulling up to the salon. He pulled into the parking spot before getting out and coming around to help me out.

"Hey, Keisha. How ya doing?" He greeted her as he walked me into the salon.

"Hey there soon-to-be-newlyweds." She replied with a huge smile.

"Hey boo." I said waddling over to sit down.

"I'll be back bae. I'm gonna go grab you some food. Keisha do you want anything while I'm out?"

"Ok babe, thanks."

"No, I'm good thanks for asking?"

"No problem, I'm out." He said before leaving.

"So, what are we doing to this head today?"

"I need a trim but I wanna do a silk press and curls. Can you pin curl it up for me and I'll take it down in the morning?"

"Ooh, that's gonna be so pretty. Well, let's get you over to the shampoo bowl so we can get started. You want to get a hydration treatment too?"

"Yeah, that's cool." About ten minutes later TC was walking through the door with my food.

"Here you go bae. Just call me when you're ready."

"Thanks again bae, I will." I said before pulling the hand sanitizer from my bag and cleaned my hands so I can eat. I opened the bag and there was a big ass club salad with ranch dressing and I couldn't wait to dig in and he even brought me a frozen strawberry lemonade to wash it down. I wasn't even mad it was a salad, the drink made up for that. I ate until the timer went off. Putting the lid back on my food, I put it back in the bag and made my way back to the shampoo bowl.

Keisha and I made small talk about everything under the sun. I called TC before she started curling my hair to tell him he can be headed back this way. About thirty minutes later my hair was all pin curled up. I pulled out my card, paid, and tipped just as TC was walking in the door.

"Looks like I'm right on time."

"Yep, we're all done here." Keisha said passing me my card back.

"How much I owe you, Keisha?"

"I already paid her bae," I answered before she could.

"Really, Yah?"

"I paid for my hair. It's no biggie babe."

"Here Keisha, put my card on file for all of her future appointments." He said doing the most as usual.

"Sure thing, give me one sec." Once she had the card set up on my file, she handed it back to him as he helped me out of the styling chair. I grabbed the rest of my food and purse from the chair it was sitting on.

"Thank you again, girl. I'll send you a picture in the morning when I take it down."

"You're welcome boo and congratulations again y'all."

"Thank you again." We said at the same time.

"I'll call you to schedule my next appointment. See you later." I told her as TC held the door open for me to walk out.

"Sounds like a plan. Enjoy the rest of y'all day."

We were back in the truck and had just pulled off from the salon when my phone started ringing.

"I don't know this number so I'm not answering it. If it's important they'll leave a message." I said sitting it on my lap as I got ready to finish eating my food. I had just stuck my fork in my salad when the phone rang again. Looking at the screen I realized it's the same number. "I wonder who keeps calling from this number. I'll call back after I finish eating."

"Yah, you never know it could be an emergency. Maybe you should answer it."

"You're right. Here you answer it while I eat." I told him as I passed my phone to him."

"Hello." He answered. "Yeah, this is TC? She's eating right now, who is this?" I could only hear his side of the conversation since I didn't tell him to put it on speaker. "Damn. Are you straight you need anything? Ok what's the room number and we will swing by in a few. Bet." He said as he ended the call.

"Who was that?" I asked after chewing my food.

"Well, if you wasn't so damn greedy and had answered the phone you would know."

"Greedy. It's your fault. You and these lil greedy babies you pumped in me." I said while laughing.

"I'll take that charge with no regrets. On a more serious note that was JuJu. She's in the hospital."

"OH MY GOD. Is he ok? I knew something bad was gonna happen, I felt that shit."

"Calm down Yah. You don't need to get yourself all worked up. He- I mean she said she is fine. She just needs a phone charger and a change of clothes. She said to check out the news because she didn't wanna say too much over the phone. I told her we would swing by later."

"The news. I wonder what the hell is going on. Let me pull up the app on my phone to see if I can find anything."

"I don't know, but I gotta feeling it has something to do with Kingston's bitch ass."

"You think so?"

"Think about it, if it didn't would she have called you? Plus, she wants us to come up there, and given the history, I don't think she would have you up there if it was even possible that Kingston would show up."

"Damn. I didn't even think about it like that. I scrolled the news app until I came across the heading *Police: Transgender woman dumped at an Ascension Parish Hospital.* I read the article aloud to TC.

"Red Maserati SUV. I told you bae. That nigga can't be not the sharpsest knife in the drawer to do some shit like that in his own damn vehicle. Then it ain't no common vehicle at that, this nigga wanna get caught."

"You think I should call Sascha and tell her what's going on so she can meet us there?"

"I don't know, Yah. JuJu might not feel comfortable with Sascha being there since they have never met, but at the same time Sascha might have some beneficial information."

"You always have all the right answers. Let me call her right now and bring her up to speed. Then, we can stop by the store and grab her some clothes and toiletries." I told him.

"Sounds like a plan. I guess we can swing by Walmart and get everything she needs at once."

"Cool babe." I said before calling Sascha and bringing her up to speed. I talked to her about five more minutes before ending the call.

"What'd she say?"

"She said she's not doing anything right now. So, she will run out to the store and get JuJu some things. Her husband will be home in a few hours and we can all meet up at the hospital about six o'clock."

"Sounds like a plan. Do you have everything you need for tomorrow morning?"

"Yeah, I'm all set. How about you?"

"As long as you're good, I'm good. We have lil time before we have to meet up at the hospital. What you wanna do til then?"

"Can we go home so I can take a quick nap? The girls are supposed to come over tonight to give me a little bachelorette party."

"Yeah, that's cool. I'll probably just hang out in my man cave so I won't be in y'all way." He said as I yawned and reclined my seat back.

"Really, Yah? You couldn't wait until we make it home?"

"I'm not sleeping babe, just resting my eyes."

"Yeah right, I'll wake you when we get home."

Chapter Twenty-Six

Shira

I have been in a constant battle with morning sickness and that bitch is winning. It seems as soon as the doctor confirmed I was pregnant, the morning sickness kicked in full speed. I don't even know why they called the shit morning sickness cause I stayed sick damn near all day long. Thank God for Osiris. I was initially pissed when he moved all of my shit out of my apartment, but that nigga has been clutch with this pregnancy shit. Everybody knows he is a little rough around the edges, but there's a side of him that most people don't get to see or even knows he possesses.

He goes above and beyond to make sure I'm good. Since most of the time I don't feel like getting out of bed. He bought a mini refrigerator that he keeps stocked up for me. It's been a process of learning what foods I can keep down and what I can't. I've also been trying natural ways to help with nausea. A few days ago, I reached out to Dr.

Pepper at BeingWell LLC. She offers many services specifically for the mind, body, and wellness. She told me to swing by she had some oils for me to help with nausea. I got a mixture of lemon and ginger oils and she instructed me to rub a few drops into my wrist and I must say it has been giving me some relief.

I'm so glad I have the kind of job that allows me to work remotely. I work as a case manager for a health insurance plan and my supervisor gave me the approval to work from home as often as I needed or permanently if I want. I appreciate the offer, but I don't think I want to permanently work from home.

"Yoooo baby mama, where you at?" Osiris loud as mouth yelled from downstairs.

I walked out of the bedroom and stood at the top of the stairs with my hands on my hips.

"Do you really have to be so extra all the time?"

"What you mean bae?"

"Wouldn't it have been easier for you to walk up here instead of standing down there yelling?"

"Not really because if I would have walked upstairs and didn't see you, I would have yelled the same thing downstairs." He said flashing that sexy-ass smile. Like the Foxx song he a *Gold Mouth Dawg* and I love that shit.

"If you say so, well what you wanted?" I asked as he made his way up the stairs.

"I was just checking on you and my seed. I see you're moving around. Are you feeling better?" Once he made it to the top, he leaned in for a kiss, sucking on my tongue before ending the kiss and leading me back into our bedroom. I sat on the bed and he sat in one of the chairs in the sitting area facing me.

"Yeah, those oils have been a big help. Anyway, what are you doing home so early?"

"That's what's up, I might need to see what other shit she got over there. Damn, I didn't know I had a set time to come home."

"Boy, bye. You're usually home by six no later than nine at night."

"I ain't have much business to handle today. For the record, I make it my business to be home a decent hour. I don't need you up stressing my baby out worrying about me in these streets all hours of the night."

"Well just shut me the fuck up. Since you home early, you wanna ride with me to go tell my mama and daddy you knocked me up?"

"I'm with it. Wait, if I didn't come home when I did you was just gonna go over there without me?"

"Yeah, I mean it's no big deal."

"Don't insult my character ma. You are not going on over there to tell ya folks something like that without me. I'm not a lame nigga. Do they even know we're together?"

"I didn't mean it like that bae. I was gonna tell them everything at once."

"You are something else. I'm pretty sure they don't know you done moved in with a nigga either, huh?"

"Nah, they don't Osiris." I responded starting to get annoyed with all of the damn questions.

"Not with that attitude. Come hop in the shower with a nigga so I can fuck some of that frustration away before we slide by ya folks." He said causing me to instantly get wet as he started pulling off his clothes before going into the bathroom. Like a dog in heat, I got my hot ass up and followed right behind him."

What was supposed to be a shower quickie turned into something else. That nigga got dick dick and he knows how to slang that shit too. Osiris is definitely the best I ever had and I think he knows it too, that's why his ass so damn cocky. We were finally on our way to my mom and dad's house an hour and a half later.

"What you so quiet for?" He asked while driving along Tiger Bend Road about five minutes away from the Shenandoah Estates where my parents lived.

"No reason. I was just wondering how they are gonna take the news."

"Look baby mama, I got you no matter what. At the end of the day, we're grown. I done been around ya folks a few times and they seem cool so I don't think they're gonna trip."

"Yeah, you're probably right. Make a right here and it's the third house on the left." I told him taking a deep breath since were about to be pulling up to my childhood home.

"Girl if you don't breathe before you pass out. You act like they gonna whip your ass or something." He told me making me laugh before he got out. He came around to my side, to open the door, taking my hand and helping me out of the car. We walked hand in hand up the driveway to the front door and knocked before I stuck my key in the door.

"Mom, dad are y'all decent in here?" I yelled from the living room while we were standing by the front door.

"Girl hush, we're in the kitchen." She yelled back.

"Damn, yo folks be freaking like that?" Osiris whispered in my ear.

"Shut up jack ass." I whispered back as we walked into the kitchen.

"Hey mama, hey daddy." I walked over to hug them. "Y'all remember Osiris?"

"Good afternoon Mr. and Mrs. Williams. How have y'all been?"

"We're good y'all, come on have a seat. We're just getting ready to eat a little supper. Y'all care to join us?"

"I thought you'd never ask." Osiris said rubbing his hands like Birdman.

"You don't even know what she cooked." I told him while laughing as we washed our hands before sitting at the table.

"What are y'all kids up to today?" My dad asked looking up at us.

"Nothing much I just wanted to come over and talk to you guys in person."

"Is everything ok baby?" My mom set the plate she was fixing down and asked.

"Yeah for the most part." She finished fixing the plates and brought them to the table two at a time. We all grabbed hands as my father blessed the food before we dug into the roast, collard greens, yams, and cornbread my mom cooked.

"So, what did you wanna talk about?" My mom asked while looking over at me.

"Well, Osiris and I are dating."

"You owe me $200, Willie." My mom shouted while we looked at them confused. "I told your father awhile back that y'all were sweet on each other. I picked up on it at one of Jackson and Erycka's parties. He said he didn't think so but I knew. So I bet him $200 that y'all would eventually end up together." She told us with a smile and holding her hand out. My dad pulled two crisp hundred dollar bills from his wallet and placed them in my mom's hand. Osiris was laughing as he looked back and forth between us.

"Y'all ain't right but that's not it. I've moved in with him and I'm almost twelve weeks pregnant."

"Pregnant? I knew somebody was pregnant. I dreamt of fish the other night but figured it was probably your sister again. My baby is having a baby." She smiled with tears in her eyes.

"Congratulations to both of you. You make sure you take care of my baby young man." My daddy said before shaking Osiris' hand. I was relieved that it with better than I expected. We sat around laughing and talking with my parents. An hour later we were gone after agreeing to let them know when my next appointment will be.

Chapter Twenty-Seven

Kingston

I just woke up after eventually falling asleep after laying in bed staring at the ceiling. Once I made it back to Burg's house, a nigga had to dick her down just to shut her the fuck up. She was all riled up about me leaving to go be with a bitch and after the shit with JuJu, I wasn't trying to hear that shit. My mind was on JuJu as I was trying to fuck all the lining out that pussy. I really felt bad and didn't mean for that shit to happen. I just hope my baby shake back and doesn't turn a nigga in to the laws.

I got up to go handle my hygiene and see what Burg had to eat. I'm just glad she had to go to work so I can get my head together and figure out my next move. I'm probably paranoid for nothing. JuJu probably woke up and didn't even mention me. I went straight to the fridge to see what I could find. There was a note stuck on the door telling me my plate was in the microwave. I grabbed the carton of orange juice outta the fridge, before going to the microwave to check out the plate. I set the microwave to warm up the blueberry pancakes, eggs, and turkey sausage she had waiting for me. I sat at the kitchen table and dug in my food and drank the juice straight from the carton. After I was done eating, I went back to the bedroom and got dressed. I grabbed my phone to see if I had any missed calls. There were no calls just a text from Burg so I clicked on it to see what she was talking about.

"Hey handsome I hope you enjoy your breakfast. Last night was wonderful, I'll call you on my lunch break."

"The food was delicious ma. Good looking out." I responded back to her before getting dressed so I can make a few moves. I got everything I needed before setting the alarm and locking up Burg's house. I hopped in my truck with no particular destination in mind and decided to go see my folks.

I could see my moms and pops sitting on the porch before I even turned in the driveway. I grabbed my phone before getting out and walking the short distance to where they were sitting.

"Hey mama, sup pops?" I said walking up the few steps to kiss my moms on her cheek and dap my daddy up.

"Hey, baby what a surprise. Are you hungry?" My moms responded first with a smile.

"What's up son? What brings you by today?" My pop asked while he looked me over.

"No ma'am. I just left Burg's she made me breakfast so I'm good. I just wanted to swing by and check y'all out." I sat on the steps stretching my legs while talking to them.

"How is Burgundi? She's such a sweet girl. That's nice of you to come by and check on us. Is everything ok with you son? It just seems like we hardly see you since you've been home."

"Yeah, she is huh? I'm good mama, just been busy trying to get back on track and stuff. I'll make it my business to try to visit more often. How does that sound?"

"Y'all are so cute together and I like her. I know it's still early but I hope you settle down with her. She would make a good wife and mother. I can't wait to have me some grandbabies."

"Aww, here you go. I'm still young and having fun mama."

"Son, fornicating is a sin. I hope you're at least wearing a raincoat. You don't need to be making no babies out of wedlock."

"Honey lay off the boy. He's a grown man and can handle himself." My dad said coming to my defense.

"And on that note, it's time for me to ride out." I said getting up dusting my pants off.

"You just got here and you're leaving already?" My mom asked looking sad.

"Well honey you didn't think mentioning him wrapping up his tallywhacker would run him off?" He asked her looking at her while I stood there laughing. I walked over and gave them both a hug after agreeing to come over for Sunday dinner, I hopped in my truck and pulled off. I decided to go home to check out the scene and see if my baby was back. I had the radio playing and was just about to get on the interstate when the noon news broadcast came on.

"Ascension Parish Sheriff's Office needs your help identifying the driver of a red Maserati SUV seen dumping a transgender woman in front of a Prairieville hospital last night. Please contact the Ascension Parish Crime Stoppers at 225-647-STOP with any information. All calls remain anonymous and you could be eligible for a tip."

I hit the brakes hard as a muthafucka and quickly busted a U-Turn. I knew I couldn't go home or back to my folks' house if they knew my truck, then they either knew it was me or were close to figuring it out. I had to go somewhere, lay low and park my fucking truck. The only place I could go was Burg's house. The only thing is I don't have a key to get inside. I said fuck it and drove to Burg's house as fast as I could without drawing attention to myself. I made it to the house, driving around the side of the house and parking in the backyard. I needed to think of something to tell her when she gets home and wanna know why the fuck I'm back here. I just hope she doesn't see, hear or read the fucking news before she gets here. I let the windows down, cut my truck off, and reclined my seat so I could figure out how the fuck I'm gonna get out of this shit. I got too much shit going on as it is and I don't need this shit right now. I still gotta get rid of that bitch MeMe.

Chapter Twenty-Eight

Tyzir

I had just wrapped up some restaurant business in my home office when I looked at the time. I knew I needed to wake Yah up now so we can hit the highway now if we wanted to avoid five o'clock traffic. I grabbed my phones and logged off my computer before leaving out of the office and going to the den where she was knocked out in the recliner sleep.

"Yah, wake up bae." I called out to her while gently shaking her.

"I'm up babe. What's wrong?" She asked with her eyes still closed.

"It's time for us to get ready to head up to the hospital if we're gonna be on time to meet Sascha at six. You know how that traffic is at five."

"Yeah, you're right. Let me go pee and freshen up a little, and then we can head on out." She said as her eyes fluttered open while she stretched before standing up."

"Ok do you need anything from upstairs?"

"Nah, I'm good I have what I need in the bathroom down here already." She had the cutest little pregnancy waddle as she walked to the bathroom. My baby is carrying three of my babies so I know I gotta come hard with her push gift. *Fuck it, I'ma get her three gifts* I thought to myself while I was in the kitchen making her a bowl of fruit to eat on the ride.

"Alright babe, I'm ready. Where are you?"

"I'm in the kitchen. I got you some fruit and a bottle of water to eat since I know you and the girls are gonna be eating some unhealthy shit later on." I told her as I put the plastic lid on the bowl before we headed out to the car. I locked up the house and helped Yah in the car, passed her the bowl of fruit, and went to the other side to get in. She had already started eating. I started the car and put her water in the cup holder before making our way to Prairieville.

"Hey, bae call your sister and let her know we are on the way to the hospital."

"Ok, I meant to do that before we left the house." She pulled her phone from her bag while balancing her bowl on her lap. I waited until she was done with her phone conversation before turning the volume up on the radio a little.

"She said they just dropped Sa'Irah off to her mother-in-law's house and were about twenty minutes away from the hospital." She told me before stuffing more fruit in her mouth.

"We'll probably be pulling up at the same time which will be before six. That means we can leave early enough for you to go home and shower before the girls get there."

"Yeah, that sounds good cause I am definitely gonna want to wash the hospital off me as soon as we get home. Why don't you, Banga and Trey go out and do something tonight?"

"It's really no big deal. I'm cool with hanging out in my man cave, but I'll hit them niggas up to see if they got anything up for the night."

We were finally pulling into the hospital and I circled the parking lot a few times before finding a spot close enough to the entrance. I got out to help Yah out, hit the alarm on my key fob and we walked hand-in-hand through the hospital doors. Yah's phone began to ring so we stepped to the side so she could answer the call.

"It's Sascha." She told me before answering the call. "Hey, Sascha, what's up? Ok, we're standing right here as soon as you walk in we'll wait for you guys." I heard her say before ending the call and putting her phone back in her bag.

"Are they here yet?"

"Yeah, she said they saw us walking in as they were parking. They should be walking in any moment now."

"There they go right there." I nodded my head towards the door when I noticed Sascha and her husband.

"Hey, y'all. This is my husband Drayke. Drayke this is my sister Mareyah and her fiance' Tyzir." Sascha said introducing everybody.

"Hi, nice to meet you. You can just call me MeMe." Yah told Drayke as she shook his hand.

"Sup, bruh? Nobody really calls me Tyzir. TC is cool." I told him as I dapped him up. He didn't say anything as he continued to look back and forth between Yah and Sascha.

"We all had the same reaction too." I told him noticing the look of shock on his face.

"Sascha told me y'all looked alike, but damn y'all are fucking identical he said. If it wasn't for the hair color I wouldn't be able to tell y'all apart," he said as we all laughed. "Congratulations on the babies."

"Thank you. Well come on y'all let's gone up here and check on the last piece of our puzzle." Yah said grabbing my hand once again as we led the way to the elevator.

"I hope he-I mean she doesn't feel like we are imposing on her." Sascha said as we rode the elevator up to the fourth floor.

"I honestly don't think it will be a problem. She already told me she wanted to meet you. I can't wait to see her reaction when she sees your face." Yah told her with a smile. We exited the elevator and made our way to room 4423 and knocked.

"Come in." JuJu's voice sounded through the door. Yah and I walked in first as she set up in bed.

"Hey sis, hey bro. Thanks for coming."

"Hey sis, are you feeling better?" Yah asked looking over her face.

"Sup, it's nothing. You're family." I sincerely told JuJu.

"Yeah, I'm feeling better and I remembered what happened to me too. Wait who's that behind you guys?" She asked finally noticing Sascha and Drayke standing behind us.

"Well, I brought someone who wanted to meet you. Despite the circumstances, I think it needed to happen at this moment." Yah told her as she stepped aside. "JuJu this here is our sister Jalisa or shall I say Sascha and her husband Drayke."

"OMG, you found her. DAMN... Y'all look just alike." She said looking back and forth between them.

"Hello, JuJu it's so nice to meet you. These are for you." She said passing the bags to her before leaning in for a hug. Drayke spoke and shook her hand before sitting in the chair by the door.

"It's so nice to meet you both. I wished we were in a better setting but I'm just glad I am alive to even be a part of this moment." She said with the biggest smile on her face. "Well why don't y'all have a seat. I'm sorry I don't have any refreshments to offer y'all." JuJu said with a serious face causing us all to bust out laughing. At least she's in good spirits.

"Well, I gave Sascha the backstory about Kingston and she has some information about him too. We'll get to that in a minute, but tell me what you remember about last night." Yah told JuJu letting her know it was cool to talk in front of them.

Chapter Twenty-Nine

JuJu

I was shocked and yet excited to see MeMe had not only found, but brought Sascha to see me. Just a few months ago I was sitting in a cell thinking about finding my biological family and today I just met my second sister. This shit is so mind-blowing if I never meet another family member, I wouldn't even care. I wonder in what order were we born. I favor them, but they are identical to each other. If it wasn't for MeMe's hair color, I would not be able to tell them apart. I had just filled them on what I remember from last night up until I blacked out.

"Well JuJu, I hate to be the bearer of bad news but your intuition was right." Sascha said pulling everyone out of their thoughts.

"Bad news? What ya mean bad news?" I asked her quite confused.

"A few weeks ago Drayke and I hosted a big party at our house. My little cousin came over with her new boyfriend Kingston."

"Kingston is a popular namem but I have a feeling you're about to tell me it's the same nigga."

"Unfortunately it is. MeMe and TC even confirmed it when I showed them pics from the party. I have them if you want to see them."

"Wheewwww chillllleeeee. I'm not even surprised about this nigga anymore. I wanna see them just to humor myself." I told her as she passed me the pics.

"Have you had a chance to talk to your cousin?" TC asked Sasha as we all got quiet to hear her answer.

"I honestly haven't. I called her a few times today, but she didn't answer. I figured she was busy at work and couldn't answer. She usually calls me back and she hasn't yet."

"This story is being reported by the news and it's possible he now knows he's a suspect. You need to get in touch with your cousin and warn her or better yet, what's her address I'll send someone over to check on her."

"I agree she needs to know that she's dealing with a monster and her life may be in danger."

"Let me try calling her again." Sascha pulled out her phone. "Where are you? Is Kingston there? Look go inside, quickly pack a bag and leave. There are some things about Kingston you don't know and I don't have time to explain right now. He is dangerous and you need to get away in case he pops up there. Burgundi I'm serious go pack a bag and come to my house. Call me back in ten minutes and let me know you are headed to my house. If you don't I'm sending the cops." We all listened to the one-sided conversation between Sascha and her cousin. I really feel sorry for her, she sounds so sweet and innocent.

"What's her address, Sascha? I'm sending my security team over just in case. I don't put shit past that nigga." TC asked her bossing the fuck up.

She called out the address as he typed it in his phone. He confirmed the address before sending a message.

"Well I hate to rush off, but I have to get home. My girls are coming over tonight for a little bachelorette gathering they're giving me tonight." MeMe stood up to let us know.

"Bachelorette? Wait are y'all getting married soon?" Sascha beat me asking the question.

"Yes, we're actually getting married at the courthouse in the morning. We'll have a big wedding later on when I'm no longer carrying three people." MeMe told us smiling wide. "I know it's short notice, but if you and your cousin are feeling up to it, I'll shoot you the address to come hang with us."

"Unt. Unt. What about me, no invite?" I asked teasing since I have to stay overnight.

"Aww boo you get well and we will hang soon. I promise."

"I would love to come sis, but I will have to pass. We gotta pick Sa'Irah up and I'm not sure what kind of mood Burgundi will be in after I explain all this shit to her." Sascha told her as she and her husband stood to leave too.

"Well, it was nice to meet you Sascha and Drayke. Thank you for the clothes and other stuff I needed. I really appreciate it."

"You're welcome and please don't hesitate to call me if you need anything. Here's my number." She handed me a piece of paper with her number on it and pulled me in for a hug.

"I know I look rough and shit, but can we take a quick picture?" I asked my sisters. MeMe wobbled over to where we were. She sat on the foot of the bed, I was in the middle and Sascha was on the other side of me. I passed my phone to Drayke so he could snap the picture."

"Ok, y'all on the count of three say J three." He directed us as we all leaned in for the picture. "One, two, three."

"J three." We all yelled at the same time like we weren't in a hospital once it clicked what the J three stood for. He snapped a few more pics of us before passing my phone back to me. They said their goodbyes and were out the door.

"Alright boo we're bout to head out too. Don't forget to call me if you need anything." MeMe said as she stood back up and grabbed her purse.

"Thank y'all again for coming and congratulations on getting married tomorrow. I already know you're gonna be a beautiful bride. Send me some pics."

"You're welcome and thank you. I got you on the pics and send me the ones we just took." Soon after saying bye they too were gone, leaving me lost in my thoughts. I turned on the TV trying to find something to watch.

"Hey baby, how are you feeling?" Nurse Lori popped in and asked.

"I'm feeling a lot better than I was this morning."

"That's good, I came by to check your vitals a little while ago, but you had visitors and I didn't want to impose."

"Yeah, that was my sisters and brothers-in-law. We're actually triplets." I told her as I smiled because it felt good to be able to finally say I have people.

Chapter Thirty

Banga

My burner phone seems to always go off at the wrong muthafuckin time. I got baby mama face down ass up while a nigga standing up in the pussy and she throwing it back like a major league all-star pitcher. Every time I try to reach for my phone, she hit me with the death grip three thousand. I did the next best thing, I pulled out and ate the pussy ass-backward she was cumming so hard she was shaking. I made sure to catch every drop before I slid my dick back in as deep I could and hitting her with deep strokes. A nigga was tap dancing on her g-spot.

"Shit Banga I'm cummmingggg." She screamed before she squirted and wet a nigga up like a muthafucking super soaker. I nutted right after hitting her with a few more strokes. She collapsed on the bed.

"Girl if you don't get up before you smash my baby." I told her once I caught my breath.

"I swear you say the most off-the-wall shit."

"How is that off-the-wall?" I asked grabbing my ringing phone.

"Don't even worry about it. I'm going take a bubble bath" She said as she stood up

"What I told you bout tryna play me like I'm some lame-ass nigga?" I told her as I walked to the bathroom and started her bubble bath. I was going through the missed calls on my burner when a text message came through with an address. I called TC on his burner to see what the fuck was up.

"Sup, bruh?" I asked as soon as he picked up.

"Nigga, I been calling you and texting you for a minute."

"My bad bruh I was handling some business."

"Look I'm leaving outta Prairieville, I just sent you an address. Kingston's bitch ass might be hiding from the laws out there."

"The fuck?"

"I don't have time to give you the full details, but you already know what I need you to do. The house belongs to a chic named Burgundi. Hopefully, she was able to get out like she was told, but if not he might be holding her hostage. She is innocent and has no idea what kinda fuck nigga he is."

"Say less. I'm bout to round up the crew and I'll hit you up once I get there." I ended the call and sent a code and the address to the crew. I went into the bathroom to turn the water off. I grabbed a towel outta the bathroom closet, turned the water on in the sink, soaping it up real good so I could wash my dick. After I was finished, I went back into the room, carried Shira to the bathroom, and gently placed her in the tub.

"I'm bout to slide baby mama. I gotta go handle some business. If I'm not back before you leave, have fun with your girls and no drinking." I told her leaning down to kiss her and sucking on her tongue before I pulled back.

"Ok bae and be safe out there. I love you."

"Love you too baby mama." I told her before I got up to go get dressed. I didn't know what I was walking into, but I made sure I was dressed to put in work. I went downstairs to the wine cellar, pulled the bottle of 1989 DOMAINE DE LA ROMANEE CONTI from its designated slot, and pressed a button opening up a secret door that no one knew about except me and TC. I grabbed a large black duffle bag and quickly loaded it with everything we may need from guns to zip ties. After zipping up the bag, I threw it over my shoulder closing the door behind me and putting the bottle back in its rightful place. I grabbed my keys off the counter once I made it back upstairs, hopped in my car, and headed to the address.

It took me about fifteen minutes to get to Mayfair and I found the house in no time. There was a gray Infinity Q50 parked in the driveway. I figured that was the chic's car, but something about the way it looked just didn't sit right with me. I noticed the way her house was positioned and that cars can drive around the side and park in the back.

I hit the block so I could scope the scene out and that's when something red in the backyard caught my attention. I couldn't really see what it was so I hit the block again going the opposite way, that way I can see the backyard from a different angle. There sitting behind the house was a red Maserati SUV which confirmed three things; the girl was in the house, Kingston was here, and I couldn't wait on the team to get here.

I parked around the corner, got out, strapped on my BRPD bulletproof vest, grabbed my cuffs, guns, and taser. I had a plug on all of the local law enforcement agencies' gear, so I don't have to worry about the cops getting called when I'm handling business. I quickly jogged around the corner to ol girl's house and walked up the driveway. Upon closer inspection of the car, I could see the door was closed but not all the way, and her purse was sitting on the passenger seat. I'm assuming she was planning to run in the house for something real quick and bust out. I couldn't see any movement in the house. I walked around back and noticed the nigga was actually in the car sleep. I backpedaled all the way back to the front door and knocked, while keeping my antennas up for him in case he woke up. She opened the door and was about to speak I put my finger up silencing her as I walked into the house and closed it behind me.

"Wh- who are you?" The slim caramel cutie with this big, wild, natural hair asked while trembling.

"You're Burgundi right?" I whispered and she nodded her head with tears in her eyes. "Listen, I'm not here to hurt you. My brother sent me on behalf of your cousin to get you safely away from here. Kingston is parked in your backyard sleep and I need you to remain calm and quiet ok?" Her eyes widened in fear as she nodded again.

"I was packing a bag like my cousin told me but got sidetracked."

"Sidetracked in a life or death situation? You are something else. Look go grab ya bag so I can get you outta here safely I told her." She ran to the back and came back with her bag, phone and keys. "Ok let's go," I told her opening the door so we could walk out and ended up being face-to-face with the devil.

"Burg, who the fuck is this nigga?" He asked with a mug on his face.

"Ol fruitcake ass nigga, don't ask her who I am like I'm not standing here. Ask me muthafucka." I told his bitch ass as I discreetly pushed her aside. I took a step back as he lunged forward just like I wanted him to. I hit him with a decent ass uppercut that dazed the fuck outta him and finished with a right hook that put his ass to sleep. I rolled him on his side, pulled his hands behind his back, and cuffed him. I pulled out my burner phone and called Guttah to see what the fuck was taking them so long.

"Say my nigga where the fuck y'all at?" I asked as soon as he answered.

"Shit, we have been blocking through this bitch looking for yo azz."

"Y'all know I'm trained to go and I had to move quickly, but pull up on me. I'm inside the house at the address I sent. Back the car as close to the front door as you can ger and pop the trunk." I told him hanging up the phone.

"You good over there ma?" I asked Burgundi as she stood against the wall terrified.

"I'm ok," she whispered.

"We bout to move this nigga and we'll be outta your way soon. You can lock up and go to your cousin's crib as planned in a few." I told her and she nodded. I heard a car pull up and opened the door as Guttah backed up to the front door. He popped the trunk before he and Sniper got out and walked to the door. I told Sniper to check his pockets for his car keys once he had them I told them to toss him in the trunk. We walked back to the front. I told Sniper to stay and advised Guttah to take the nigga back to the warehouse. Once he pulled off Sniper and I walked back to the front door.

"Alright baby girl. You can go lock up now and head by your people."

"Thank you so much. Wait you never told me your name."

"It's not important. Just call me Jigga City's Finest." I said causing her to smile for the first time since I had been in her presence.

"Well thank you again Mr. Jigga City's Finest and who are you?" She turned to Sniper and asked.

"You can just call me Sniper baby." He told her as smiled flashing his diamond grill. We waited until she locked up her house and had pulled off before we walked around the corner to my car. We bent a few corners killing time until it was dark enough for us to go back so Sniper can get the car outta the backyard. Once we got the car, we drove it to an abandoned lot in the South not too far from the warehouse.

Chapter Thirty-One

Mareyah

I had so much fun with my girls last night. We pigged out on good food and drinks, well mine and Shira's were virgins after she revealed she was pregnant. We played a few games and just caught up on everything going on in each other's lives. Aside from Monique, I hadn't had a chance to tell everyone else about the Sascha and JuJu. I wish I had recorded their reactions when I told them about Kingston being JuJu's boyfriend. They were all familiar with the news story, but had no idea it was Kingston they were looking for and of course I had to tell them about him messing with Sascha's lil cousin. I swear if this wasn't my life and someone had told me this story, I wouldn't even believe it.

I was glad TC got outta the house instead of sitting alone in his mancave. He and Banga hung out, but I got a feeling it had something to do with Kingston. I got up to shower and take care of my hygiene before going downstairs for breakfast. I moisturized my skin, slipped on a matching bra and panty set, before throwing on my robe and tying it. My dress and shoes were already downstairs so I grabbed my phone and purse before going downstairs.

"Good morning babe." I told TC as I walked into the kitchen where he was fixing our plates.

"Morning bae." He said as he turned and kissed me on my forehead. I took a seat at the island while he poured us each a glass of orange juice before sitting down in front of me.

"Today's the big day." I said excitedly that I was finally marrying the love of my life.

"I can't wait to make you Mrs. Cunard. Are you nervous?"

"Nervous, hell no. I can't wait to become Mrs. Cunard." I told him before said grace and ate our food. I got up once were done to use the bathroom and brush my teeth again. I heard the doorbell and figured it was my make-up artist. I came out just as TC was showing Brittney with Bei

Pretty Artistry to the room where she can set up and I waddled in behind them.

"Good morning girl." I greeted her as I told her.

"Good morning boo. Congratulations and look at that bump."

"Thank you boo. They're growing so fast I feel like I'm running out of room."

"I can only imagine. You are definitely glowing hunty." She said as I sat down so we can get started. She beat my face to perfection before and took a few after pics and videos to post to her social media pages. TC paid and tipped her before she left. My mama was adamant that she and my dad came over so she could help me get dressed and I could ride with them to the courthouse. TC went upstairs to get dressed so he didn't see me in my dress. About thirty minutes later, I had taken the pin curls aloose and had my hair styled the way I wanted. I was dressed and snapped a few pics to send to Keisha before we left . It didn't take us long to get to the courthouse. My daddy let us out in the front while he went to park. We went inside and ran into Monique and Shay, shortly after my daddy, Shira, and Banga walked in talking to each other.

"Morning everybody, you look beautiful sis." Banga said as he walked closer to us.

"Morning y'all thanks, bro. Where's my soon-to-be husband?"

"That nigga standing in the front. I told him I'll come get him when it's time."

"You can go get him now, we're next anyway. My dad insisted on walking me down the aisle to where the judge was standing and everybody filed in behind us. He placed my hand inside of TC's before going to stand next to my mom. We stood facing each other with tears in our eyes. I was literally on cloud nine and don't even remember saying *I DO*.

"By the power vested in me and the State of Louisiana, I now pronounce you husband and wife. You may now kiss your bride." We kissed for what felt like forever before coming up for air. "Ladies and gentlemen, I present to you Mr. and Mrs. Tyzir

Kahmal Cunard." Everyone clapped and cheered, we signed the license along with Banga and Monique as our witnesses before we left out of the courtroom. Once we were all in the lobby, mama announced that she had a catered brunch setup and for everyone to follow them to their house.

"I told you my mama was gonna put something together." I said once we were in TC's car and heading to my parents' house.

"It's cool Yah. You're their only child. You better enjoy it because once the babies get here, you're gonna be old news to them."

"Whatever. I just didn't think it made sense with the baby shower next week." I said hunching my shoulders.

"Well, let's go in and make the best of it." He said before getting out and coming to help me out. Once we got inside, everything was simply decorated but yet still beautiful. There was a photographer, arch, and backdrop set up in the sitting room for us to take pictures. We took plenty of pictures, ate, cut the cake, laughed, and talked before finally leaving. I couldn't wait to get home and get dicked down for the first time as a married woman.

I don't know if it was the pregnancy or the excitement of being married but once we got home, I was taking off my clothes as I was walking through the door.

"Damn Yah, I see what type of time you on." TC said as he unbuttoned his shirt. He picked me up, sat me on the island, and spread my legs as wide as he could. He pulled up a seat, diving headfirst, he licked and slurped like he was eating watermelon.

When he finally pulled away, he looked like a glazed Krispy Kreme doughnut and I leaned down to kiss him and taste my sweetness at the same time. He stood up, undid his pants and I pulled his boxers down, that dick bounced out like it was on hydraulics. That thang was thangin and my mouth was watering.

"Sit me in the chair babe." I told him never taking my eyes off that meat.

"You sure Yah? I'm good either way."

"Yeah, I'm sure." Once he sat me in that chair, I was at eye level with his dick, I moved my hair out my face and went to work. I spit on his dick before swallowing it with no hands until it was touching the back of my throat. I relaxed before I started humming on it just the way he liked it and used one of my hands to massage his balls. I pulled his dick out jacking it with my hand till I saw that vein pulsing before I started back sucking it like it was a green apple blow pop.

"Damn it Yah." He said grabbing a handful of my hair. "Ease up bae, I'm bout to cum." He was trying to pull away so he wouldn't cum in my mouth. Certain things he didn't feel comfortable doing since I was pregnant. I slowly eased his dick out of my mouth, he stood me up and walked me over to the wall placing my back against it. He lifted one of my legs as he entered me in one swift motion. He lifted my other leg, wrapping them both around his waist as he delivered deep upward thrusts. Our bodies moved in sync to the beat of our own drum. My juices ran out of me as he continuously hit my spot.

"Oooooooohhhhhh babe." I moaned out as my eyes rolled into the back of my head. We always have some bomb sex, but this was some next-level shit. The dynamic of our connection was deeper than ever before, I could feel our souls tying.

"Aaaaaaahhhhhhhh I'm cummminggggggg." I screamed out cumming harder than I had ever came in my life. I swear I was seeing stars and he was still stroking. I came three more times back-to-back before he finally pulled out and nutted on my belly. He slowly eased me down onto the chair as we both caught our breath. He went upstairs and ran me a bath so I could relax. Once my legs regained feeling I went upstairs and got in the tub while he went downstairs to clean up our mess. I was finishing up my bath, getting ready to rinse when he came up to shower. After going another round in the shower, we washed up, rinse, and got ourselves ready for bed.

“Good night Mrs. Cunard. I love you.” He said kissing my temple as we cuddled in bed.

“Good night Mr. Cunard. I love you more.” I told him as I looked up into his eyes and smiled.

Chapter Thirty-Two

Kingston

I can't believe I got caught slipping like that. I planned to hide in the back of Burg's house until she came home from work, but somehow I fell asleep. Imagine my surprise when I woke up, only to get to the front of the house to see her and some nigga about to walk out. The nigga knocked me on my ass so fast, I don't even know if she ever answered when I asked her who he was. I had been holed up at some kinda warehouse ever since he snatched me up. I don't even know this nigga or what the fuck he wanted with me.

The nigga didn't say shit, he just made sure I was hogtied before he tossed me in this dark ass room where I had been ever since. I don't even have the energy to try to think of a way to escape. I guess the good thing about it is he got me and not the police. I'll go to hell before I go back to jail. I was tryna figure out if Burg set me up and what's her connection to this nigga.

"Yeah bring his bitch ass out here." I heard someone say before I was yanked up off the floor where I was sitting. He brought me in another room where there was MeMe's nigga and the nigga who snatched me up from Burg's house.

"Look at his switch hitter ass. You could see the wheels turning in his head." The nigga told MeMe's nigga while looking at me. MeMe's nigga tapped on the window of a room that I assumed was an office. I could have collapsed when I focused on everybody as they walked out one by one, MeMe, JuJu, Burg, and Burg's cousin Sascha. I looked at them curious as fuck wondering what the hell is going on.

"Yah would you like to go first?" The nigga asked as I looked around wondering who the fuck is Yah.

"Yeah babe, let me get this over with so I can get ready for my baby shower." She responded to her nigga. "Kingston, I really wanna say some mean and ugly things to you, but I don't want to transfer that energy to my babies. I will say this because of your actions, I was able to find out some very valuable information. You see JuJu, your jailhouse lover turned girlfriend, Sascha and I are triplets. You already know Burgundi and Sascha are cousins and everybody is now aware of the shit you were doing behind their backs. JuJu wanted to end things with you when I told her the reason you were locked up, but figured it was best to continue to play the role and moved in with you anyway. You messed up when you put your hands on her and then drove your own car to dump her in front of the hospital. You really are as dumb as a box of rocks." She called herself preaching to me like she was their spokesperson. I was shocked as hell to find out these muthafuckas were actually triplets and were now connected because of me. I kept saying they favored each other.

"I don't care what happens to you, but I'm pretty sure we all know your fate. I do feel like out of all of us standing here you owe Burgundi an apology the most. I don't need one. You manipulated her and intentionally forced her into a relationship with a gay man, without her knowledge and that can be damaging to a woman's mental. I hope you rot in hell." She finished her lil speech.

"Fuck you bitch. Fuck all you bitches." I yelled out not giving a fuck about none of the shit she was saying.

"You better watch ya mouth before I cut your tongue out and stuff it down your throat." Her nigga said to me as he mugged the fuck outta me. "Anybody else wanna say anything?" He asked the rest of em. They all shook their heads no. "Alright bae, y'all go ahead and get out of here. I'll meet you at the house before the shower." He said kissing her on the lips. I can't lie she still looked bad as fuck even with that big ass belly. I can't believe I fucked three out of the four females standing in front of me and the one I really loved the most was JuJu. I was feeling bad about what happened and this bitch was planning on leaving me. That shit hurt a nigga heart. Once they were gone, the nigga from Burg's house brought me a notepad and a pen.

"Look nigga copy this letter word for word. If you try any funny shit, I will remove each and every one of your fingers one by one with this muthafukin ice pick." He told me pointing it at me sending chills down my spine. I did what he said realizing I was writing my suicide note. *Damn, I really came home and fucked up my entire life,* I thought as I continued to write. Once I was finished, he used his gloved hands to rip the note from the pad and stuffed it in an envelope. "Just so you know, I'm the plug you could never get in touch with nigga and I was never gonna put ya bitch ass on." He said loud enough and everyone started laughing around me. Then it hit me this must be that nigga Banga, JB was telling me about.

"You know, I had been trying to figure out the best way to kill a hoe ass nigga like you after you snatched up my pregnant wife and boy did I have some shit planned for you. That is until the shit you pulled with JuJu you got to be the dumbest muthafucka alive to dump somebody in front of a hospital driving a red Maserati. Shit for all that, you should have just parked and walked her inside the hospital."

"Fuck you nigga. You married my leftovers."

"Leftovers? That's all yo bitch ass could come up with? You see Yah was way too much woman for you and you couldn't handle her."

"Yeah, that nigga prefer his women with a little T.A.D." Banga said while laughing.

"What the fuck is T.A.D. bruh?" MeMe's nigga asked him.

"T.A.D. nigga. Titties, ass, and dick." He said falling over laughing.

"Bruh you ignant yeah. Let's go ahead and take this nigga to go push his own shit back. I gotta get home and get dressed for the shower." He told the nigga Banga who nodded to the nigga who brought me out here. The nigga stuffed a gag in my mouth before lifting me from the chair and walking me to the back of a van they had waiting outside. Banga stuffed the envelope with the note I had just wrote in my pocket before the other nigga tossed me in the back of the van.

"We gon follow y'all my nigga." A voice from the front of the van said. Soon we were moving, I didn't know how much time I had so I did the only thing I could think to do. I prayed. Something I haven't done in a long time. I prayed for forgiveness. I asked the Lord to forgive me for everything I did to MeMe, JuJu, and even Burg. Since the secret is out, I just pray my family isn't ashamed of me and I didn't break my mama's heart. I've known since middle school I was gay and had been hiding the shit for years. I always kept a bad bitch even before MeMe and many times fantasized about a man while fucking them. I just knew I couldn't disappoint my parents by telling them I was gay.

After a few minutes of driving, the van came to a stop. I heard two doors open, followed by footsteps. A different nigga from the one who threw me in the van opened the door and yanked me out. He walked me to my car where the other one was holding the driver's side door open. Banga and Meme's nigga was standing with their guns aimed at my head. The nigga uncuffed me while the other one went around to the passenger side and got in. Once he was in the car, the other nigga pushed me in the driver's seat and closed the door while pointing his gun at me through the window. I was ready to get this shit over with and had made peace with my fate during the ride.

"Look nigga, when I put this piece in your hand, put it up to your head and pull the fucking trigga." The nigga in the car with me said. I looked over at him with tears in my eyes and noticed he had an iced-out diamond grill in his mouth. "Don't start that ol pussy ass crying and shit. You ready to get this over with?" He asked and I nodded my head. After he passed the gun to me, I closed my eyes and placed it to my temple before squeezing the trigger. *BOOM.*

Chapter Thirty-Three

Tyzir

I made it home in time to shower and get dressed for the baby shower. Yah and I were instructed to wear all white. She had on a custom-made sexy, lace halter maternity dress that fit snug around her belly and flowed down into a little train behind her. I helped her put on a pair of gold sandals to match her gold accessories. Her hair was cascading in curls, pulled to one side and flowing over her left shoulder. My wife is the most beautiful woman in Baton Rouge. She was standing in the mirror checking herself out and I was snapping off-guard pics of her with my phone.

Once we were dressed, we climbed in my truck and headed to the St. Gabriel Community Center where the baby shower was being held. It didn't take us long to get there and when we pulled up there were cars everywhere. Yah looked around the parking lot in awe at the number of people that were here to celebrate our babies.

"I can't wait to go in here and see what they came up with." She said with a smile.

"Well let's go check it out." I told her turning the truck off, getting out, and going around to help her out. Both of our mouths dropped to the floor as soon as I opened the door.

The pink and blue princess and prince theme was dope as fuck. Once again, Candie had snapped on the fucking decorations. The colors were pink, blue, and white. There was a backdrop with two black princes wearing blue and a black princess wearing pink. The gift tables blew my mind there were three long tables completely filled with gifts on top and under them. There was a beautiful treat table filled with an assortment of theme matching treats made by Róial Kreations. Once again, Linda's Catering was on the food and she did not disappoint. I looked around at all the people who came out to support us and was amazed. Who would've thought a baby shower would bring the city out like this?

"Come on babe, let's go grab our seat." I told her walking her to the front of the room where the white and gold regal sofa sat in front of the backdrop surrounded by a balloon arch and decorative boxes that spelled the word baby out.

We enjoyed our shower from beginning to end. The games, the food, the people, just everything. Even Banga participated and played a few games. The guests were all sent home with treats, souvenirs, and a to-go box of food since there was so much food leftover. Yah's OG was smart and had rented a U-Haul this time for all of the gifts. Once we loaded the truck up, Yah's folks, Shira and Banga followed us home to unload everything.

"Did you enjoy yourself, bae?" I asked her as we were driving home.

"Yes, everything was beyond beautiful. Mama and the girls did a really good job with everything."

"I can't lie, they did a damn good job." As we were riding there was a breaking news alert that came on the radio. *Body of a man found in vehicle with an apparent self-inflicted gunshot wound in South Baton Rouge. The vehicle is believed to be the one involved in the recent dumping of a trans woman in front of an Ascension Parish Hospital.*

"Damn." Yah whispered.

"You good?"

"Yeah, I knew it was gonna happen, but I didn't think it would be suicide."

"It was bound to happen. He was fighting too many demons." I told her not volunteering any more information and we drove the rest of the way home in silence.

We pulled into the garage and I helped her in the house and upstairs. She said she wanted to take a bath and go to bed. I could tell she was exhausted from today and needed to relax. I ran her a warm bubble bath and helped her get in before going down to help unload the truck. It took us a minute to get everything put upstairs in the guest rooms for now. Once everybody was gone, I went upstairs to check on Yah and she was in bed sleeping. I poured myself a shot of D'Usse and threw it back before going to get in the shower. I climbed in bed behind Yah and went straight to sleep.

The next week, Yah had a nigga cleaning and putting up baby stuff until there was no more room in the nursery. We had to leave everything else in the guest rooms until we needed it. I can't wait till my babies get here and fill this house up with some noise. We were relaxing in the den when Yah got up to go to the bathroom. Soon as she stood up there was a gush of fluid that shot out of her making a puddle beneath her and her eyes got big ass hell.

"Babe I think my water just broke." She quietly while standing in place.

"Are you sure you didn't pee on yourself?" I asked just to be sure.

"I'm sure. Owww." She said grabbing her stomach and bending over. "That contraction just confirmed it. I'm gonna go take a shower. Can you put the bags in the car and make me a sandwich please?" She walked off without a care in the world down the hall to the full bathroom to get in the shower. I got up grabbed the mop and cleaned up the floor and the trail Yah left on the way to the bathroom. I washed my hands and made her sandwich before going get all of our bags and putting them in the truck. I went back inside to check on Yah and she was just getting out of the shower. I rubbed her down with body butter and helped her put on her dress and slides.

"How are you feeling?"

"I'm scared shitless, but trying to remain calm and time these contractions. I honestly thought we had a few more weeks."

"I know bae, I thought we did too, but you know I got you no matter what." I told as I kissed her softly trying to calm her down. "Come on let's get you in the truck." I told her leading her to the garage. I helped her get in the truck, started it up, went back inside to get her sandwich and a bottle of water, locked up the house, and made my way back to the truck.

The ride to the hospital was quiet as she ate her sandwich and I made a mental note on having to put a rush on one of her push gifts. I figured since she was giving me three babies she deserves three gifts. It took me a while to decide on what I wanted to get her but I eventually came up with a vacation to Punta Cana, a surprise wedding, and a mommy mobile. I got her a cocaine white 2020 Cadillac Escalade customized with upgrades and monogrammed seats. I'll just email the dealership and tell them I need it sooner than originally discussed.

We arrived at Woman's Hospital and went inside to let them know Yah was in labor and her contractions were now a minute apart. They rushed out to the truck with a wheelchair to come and get her. I grabbed our bags, passed my keys to the valet, got the ticket, and ran inside to be with my wife. Once they had Yah in bed and hooked to a bunch of machines and monitors, we waited on Dr. Henderson to come in and check her out he said surprisingly she can move forward with her plans for a natural vaginal birth. She was already at eight centimeters so I knew it wouldn't be long.

I sent out a group message to let everybody know what was going on and give them all the information. Mama Erycka called instead of texting back to let us know they were getting ready to head up here to the hospital. I couldn't respond to the texts since I had to get ready for the delivery. They had moved her to an operating room just in case she may need a c-section. Shit, a nigga was nervous as a muthafucka when I stepped in the room. There was so many nurses, doctors, equipment, and anything else they needed.

I was standing by Yah feeding her ice chips as she squeezed my hand during each contraction. About ten minutes later the doctor came back to check her again and she was now ten centimeters it was time to get this show on the road.

Chapter Thirty-Four

Mareyah

On September 16, 2019, at seven forty-seven, seven fifty-nine, and eight-fifteen pm, I gave birth to my babies Tyzir Kahmal Cunard Jr., Tyriz Karsen Cunard, and Marleyah Me'Yhari Cunard. Tyzir was three pounds, twelve ounces, and sixteen point nine inches long, Tyriz was three pounds, ten ounces, and sixteen point six inches long, and Marleyah was three pounds, eight ounces, and sixteen point three inches long. Our boys were identical and looked just liked TC and little Miss Marleyah was my twin. The hospital staff was calling them The Cunard Three since they were not only born vaginally, but had passed all of their tests, which is extremely rare.

We had been home for about three weeks now and I thank God for my support system. My parents had literally been here every day helping us out and most nights they stayed. Banga and Shira came by as much as possible to get their practice for when they have their baby. Cardell is currently in rehab so Monique would come by to clean, help with the babies, or whatever we needed her to do. Shay worked a lot during the week so she came on weekends to help out as well. I couldn't fathom how we would have managed without their support. Sascha and JuJu were even pitched in when they could.

"Good morning bae." TC came into the room with a breakfast tray. "Go ahead and eat up. I'll start getting the babies ready for their appointment."

"Thanks babe. I laid their clothes out last night next to their cribs. Are they still sleeping?"

"Slugger is wide awake looking around." He said calling Tyriz by the nickname we gave him since he is always swinging his little balled-up fist.

"Do you need me to feed him before you put his clothes on him?"

"I gave him one of the bottles you pumped since you were sleeping when he woke up. I got him, you just eat and get yourself together." He told me kissing my forehead as he walked back to the nursery.

We were home alone trying to get used to caring for the babies by ourselves for a bit. Last night was the first night that it was just the two of us and I must say we did well. The babies were all down at the same time for bed. They all woke up at around three in the morning for a feeding and a diaper change. We both got up and tagged teamed with getting them all fed and changed.

I had just finished with my food when I heard crying on the baby monitor. I got up to go and help TC. When I made it to the nursery, he had Slugger dressed in his navy blue onesie with *Mama's Little Prince* on the front in white letters, matching navy blue cap and white socks. He laid him back in his crib and was turning towards Jr. when Leyah started fussing.

"I'll get Jr. babe, you can get Leyah." I told him to make his decision easier. It's no secret that Leyah is already a spoiled daddy's girl. I took a seat in the rocker and pulled out my breast to feed Jr. He struggled with latching on at first, but he has gotten so much better.

"I think we did pretty good for our first night alone bae." TC said sitting in the rocker feeding Leyah.

"Yeah, I was just thinking the same thing before I came in here."

"I want you to know that any support you need whether it be a nanny, housekeeper, time to yourself, or whatever, I got you." He said reminding me that my well-being is a priority to him.

After burping Jr. I got him dressed in the exact same outfit as Slugger and laid him in his crib. TC had Leyah dressed in her matching onesie dress that was white, trimmed in navy blue, with *Daddy's Little Princess* in Navy blue letters, navy blue socks, and a navy blue headband. Once we had all of the kids laying in their cribs, we went to get ourselves showered and dressed as quickly as possible. Twenty minutes later we were loading up the kids in my mommy mobile, I snapped a few pics and we were on our way to their four-week-old appointment.

Their appointment went pretty good, up until they had to get their shots. I cried more than my babies did and TC had to calm me down. Their pediatrician said they were right on track with their growth and development. We changed all of their diapers and fed them before we loaded them back in the truck for the drive home. They were all knocked out sleep after driving about five minutes and I just looked at my babies in awe. Being a mom is a different kind of love and I'm just so blessed to be theirs. I turned and caught TC staring at me in the rearview mirror.

"The shock still hasn't worn off yet, huh?" He quietly asked not wanting to wake them.

"Nah, and I don't think it ever will."

"I know right. It feels so good to have the sounds of something we created out of love filling up the house."

"Yesssss. I agree babe. Out of all things that happened this year, becoming your wife and giving birth to these three little miracles are both tied for the best day of my life."

Once we got home, we got the babies settled in their Mamaroos in the den and turned the TV to cartoons. I went upstairs to change into something more comfortable. When I came back downstairs, I peeped in on the babies and they were just cooing and watching TV. I went into the kitchen where TC was standing at the stove cooking something. I hugged him from behind and rested my head on his back. He stopped what he was doing and turned to face me.

"Sup, bae? You good?" He asked pulling me in closer for a hug resting his hands on my ass.

"Yeah, I just wanted to be close to you for a moment. What you in here cooking?"

"I know bae. It seems like these days we always have a baby in our arms. Shrimp tacos, you hungry?"

"I can definitely eat." I told him smiling.

"Greedy ass." He said laughing. We sat at the island eating our food and talking before going back in there with the babies. We took them out of the Mamaroos and put them in their carriers to take them upstairs for their baths. After getting them all bathed and fed, we put them in their cribs and went into our bedroom. I ran us a bubble bath and we just relaxed and enjoyed each other while listening to the sounds of our beautiful creations.

Epilogue

One Year Later

Mareyah

TC did an amazing job with my push gifts. He took it upon himself to hire a wedding planner to take care of everything for our wedding and I am thankful that he did. There is no way I could have planned a wedding while tending to three babies. He took care of everything and not once did I have any idea that he had this surprise waiting on me. I can't wait to go on our honeymoon in Punta Cana either. A vacation is long overdue and much needed.

I still haven't gone back to work at the hospital and I honestly have no desire to. I love being a full-time housewife and mother. I did take TC up on his offer for a nanny/housekeeper, but once the news spread about the Coronavirus pandemic, we didn't allow anyone in our house. We were in quarantine like everybody else and we figured out a system to maintain our house, the kids, and our sanity. It was so hard not being around our family and friends, Zoom and FaceTime became our best friends.

The wedding is being held at Elegant Affairs a beautiful venue in Gonzales. The colors are emerald green, rust, ivory, and gold and our entire wedding party looked fly as fuck. JuJu and Alannah were my bridesmaids and wore emerald green dresses, Shira and Shay were the maids of honor and wore rust dresses, and Monique and Sascha were the matrons of honor and wore gold dresses. Banga and Trey were TC's best men. Darren and Drayke were groomsmen, Cardell was stuck in rehab due to the pandemic and was just able to come home a few weeks ago.

Everyone had walked down the aisle and it was now my turn. I stood up when I heard the instrumental to Ledisi's *Anything For You* begin. I walked out and started singing as I walked down the stairs where my dad was waiting for me. I sang my heart out as I walked down the aisle to my husband. My focus was on him and him only, and by the time

I got to him we were both in tears just like the first time. The ceremony only took thirty minutes and for the rest of the night, we partied. We were not just celebrating ourselves, we were celebrating being alive. All of our guests were required to wear masks. The triplets were walking and were all over the place. The highlight was seeing our god daughter, Banga, and Shira's baby girl, Orisha for the first time in person. August 8, 2020, our one-year wedding anniversary is a day I will never forget.

My sisters and I have developed a bond that was so amazing. My family and friends gladly welcomed them into our circle. JuJu is doing so much better. Since Shira's old apartment was empty and she needed a place to stay, she was able to move in and take over the lease. We hooked her up with a job at Cunard's and she is an amazing worker. She recently learned how to drive, and bought her first car, a 2020 bright red Camaro. Her lawyer called her yesterday to inform her she had won her lawsuit against the prison for a settlement of four and a half million dollars. She was so excited because she can now pay for her operation and buy her a house.

Sascha and I are thick as thieves too and Sa'Irah loves being a big cousin. She FaceTimes them all day every day. Drayke is cool with the rest of the guys, at first they weren't too sure but he has seemed to prove himself to them over time. The pandemic but a damper on their guys' nights and shit but as the restrictions are being lifted, there will be more in the future.

As for me, Kingston's suicide definitely provided me with the closure I needed. I no longer have to worry or constantly look over my shoulder in fear. I am alive, happily married, with three beautiful children, extremely blessed and I owe it all to the Baton Rouge Boss That Saved My Heart.

The End

Made in the USA
Monee, IL
23 July 2021

74190155R00164